Marginal Voices

The Texas Pan American Series

Marginal Voices

Selected Stories by
Julio Ramón Ribeyro

English translation by
Dianne Douglas

Foreword by Dick Gerdes

UNIVERSITY OF TEXAS PRESS   AUSTIN

Requests for permission to reproduce material from this work should be sent to
Permissions, University of Texas Press, Box 7819, Austin, TX 78713-7819.

∞The paper used in this publication meets the minimum requirements of American
National Standard for Information Sciences—Permanence of Paper for Printed Library
Materials, ANSI Z39.48-1984.

Library of Congress Cataloging-in-Publication Data

Ribeyro, Julio Ramón, date
    [Palabra del mudo.   English.   Selections]
    Marginal voices : selected stories / by Julio Ramón Ribeyro ; English translation by
Dianne Douglas — 1st ed.
    p.   cm. — (The Texas Pan American Series)
    ISBN 978-0-292-77058-4
    I. Title.   II. Series.
PQ8497.R47P313   1993
863-dc20   92-30359

Contents

Foreword
by Dick Gerdes

*J*ulio Ramón Ribeyro, a native of Peru, was born in the capital city of Lima in 1929. Ribeyro, the author of some eight volumes of short stories (well over 100 stories in all), many of which have been published collectively in three volumes entitled *La palabra del mudo* (Reticences, Lima 1972/1977), has also written novels, plays, and literary criticism. The translator of the present volume chose fifteen stories written between 1952 and 1975, taken from *La palabra del mudo*. Other modern Peruvian writers—Ciro Alegría (1909–1967), José María Arguedas (1911–1969), and Mario Vargas Llosa (1936–)—also started out writing short stories, but they quickly turned to the novel as their preferred genre. While Ribeyro has tried his hand, and successfully, too, at writing novels, in forty years of uninterrupted writing he has remained faithful to the short story genre. Asked what it means to write a short story and how to define it, Ribeyro states that "a la postre no sé lo que es, aparte de un texto en prosa de extensión relativamente corta. En este texto puede entrar lo que sea . . . un recuerdo de infancia, comunicar un sueño, llevar una idea hasta el absurdo, trascribir un diálogo escuchado en un café, proponerle al lector un acertijo o resumir en una alegoría su visión del mundo" [in the end, I don't know what it is, except a relatively short prose text. It can be based on anything . . . a childhood memory; it can retell a dream, take an idea to absurd extremes, transcribe a dialogue heard in some café, propose a riddle to the reader or synthesize a vision of the world in an allegory].

The short story genre in Peru has a long history; antecedents are found in the sketches of local color by Felipe Pardo y Aliaga (1806–1868), the "tradición," a short story hybrid of colonial and romantic local color by Ricardo Palma (1833–1919), the Modernist stories by Abraham Valdelomar (1888–1919), and indigenist themes of protest in the narratives of Ciro Alegría and José María Arguedas. By the early 1950s, however, Peruvian short narrative had exhausted itself in terms of content and style. Rural indigenous themes had dominated for over forty years because of the urgent need to expose the realities of the human condition of the majority of Peru's Indian and mestizo populations, in order to bring them to the attention of Peru's mainly white, educated, non-Indian coastal population, which was basically unfamiliar with the country's marginalized Andean masses. Early on, massive migration to Peru's coastal cities, particularly Lima, had created serious socioeconomic problems that have gone unabated ever since.

The beginning of Ribeyro's writing career in 1952 coincides with his departure a year later for Europe, where he has lived ever since. While Ribeyro continues to make brief trips back to Peru on an irregular basis, there is no doubt that his stories in many ways have been deeply affected by this separation from his homeland. However, the result has hardly been negative; in fact, the perspectives Ribeyro creates in his stories, as in the case of Jorge Luis Borges, with whom Ribeyro has strong affinities, have been continually honed by this distancing effect between writer and reality, which means basically not being there, or not actually seeing, but instead, remembering and recreating. Consequently, Ribeyro has tightly juxtaposed elements of descriptive reality and fantasy, creating a sinewy internal tension in his stories that suggests the influence of the old masters and the presence of modern perspectives on life, as seen through the eyes of a writer firmly grounded in the historical and social situation and collective attitudes of his native Peru, particularly during the 1940s and 1950s. This was a time when he and other writers of his generation began to discover those new urban realities and to focus on the serious, burgeoning problems of migration, urban expansion, slums, discrimination, and violence in modern Peru.

Writing from the marginalized position of the exiled writer in Europe, Ribeyro takes social commentary, applies an overlay of minute detail, sharp observation, and biting irony, and brings it to life by enveloping his characters in fantastic elements, much in the way Borges uses the double, Juan José Arreola plays with enigma and paradox, or Franz Kafka creates the eccentric and the bizarre. The subtle combination of social commentary and fantasy in Ribeyro's narrative works makes his stories peculiar, different, attractive, engaging, and contemporary. Ribeyro's stories provide a good read mainly because of the use of psychological aspects in the characterization, resulting in the creation of a distinctive tone that exudes a philosophical attitude about contemporary urban life. His characters are those who belong to the faceless anonymity of the big city, where the banality of simple lives is played out in private and public places like hotel rooms, boarding houses, dives, offices, houses, streets, and parks. In these settings—some in Europe, some in Peru—Ribeyro sets into motion the development of a common, arbitrary incident that, lacking any logic or apparent causality, pits the frail individual hopes of success and happiness against the harsh realities of individual failure: that one grows old, that there is no way to hold back time, that many people cannot communicate with each other, or that reality is absurd. In this vein, there is something totally Peruvian in these stories; it is the atmosphere of a modern-day urban malaise, a generalized feeling of melancholy, sadness, pessimism, and alienation that invades his stories, saturating them with feelings of resignation and failure. This is coupled to a futile attempt to rescue nostalgically from the ashes of bygone days the meaning in life.

Such is the case in "Alienation," a story about racism, discrimination, and the vulnerability of false values in Peru as seen from the perspective of Roberto López, a person of color who desperately tries to become white and to assume a new identity. In typical Ribeyro fashion, the first sentence of the story sums up its significance: "A pesar de ser zambo y de llamarse López, quería parecerse cada vez menos a un zaguero de Alianza Lima y cada vez más a un rubio de Filadelfia" [Despite being a sambo and having the name López, he wanted to look less like a person who plays defense on the Alliance Lima team and more like a blond from Philadelphia]. Conflict is set into motion through the oppositions of reality-fantasy, sambo-white, Lima-Philadelphia; the nuclear verb "want to look like" implies from the beginning the impending result: inferiority, anguish, and failure. Calling the story a parable, the narrator describes the sad process in which Roberto becomes Bobby, ends up joining the U.S. Army and dying in Korea, after which, ironically, his mother's attempts to collect on an insurance policy are thwarted. A subtheme in the story deals in parallel fashion with an upper-class white girl from Lima who eventually marries an American and lives a life of banality and misery in a small hamlet in Kentucky.

In another story, "The Insignia," the first-person narrator retells how he found a strange insignia in a garbage heap on the street. That seemingly insignificant event totally alters his life, for the insignia represents a wealthy international sect of which he becomes a member. Years pass, and the narrator, unable to explain what has happened to him, can only suggest that any explanation would have to be based on some doctrine of the occult. As a final example, "Bottles and Men" recreates that unfortunate and sad situation when father and son, now older, meet up after not seeing each other for many years. The encounter leads the reader through the ephemeral joys and excitement of such a reunion and ends in a fight when the father describes what really happened to his son's mother, giving an explanation unacceptable to the son. Seeing himself reflected in his father's face, he kicks the old man in the stomach, steps over him, and leaves. Feelings of desperation, humiliation, anger, and sadness pervade the ending of the story.

Collectively, Ribeyro's stories create a distinctive tone of melancholic pessimism that captures in ironic fashion the banality, absurdity, and anguish of a middle-to-lower-class fake bourgeoisie that has no place in Peruvian society; it is a class without any history, traditions, future, or identity. However, Ribeyro probes his characters' psyches from a position of compassionate skepticism that, again, creates a special tone of irony and resulting melancholy in his stories. Herein lies the beauty of Ribeyro's narratives: the striking juxtaposition of the characters' private, intimate illusions of success and the harsh reality of failure, melancholy, and pathos. In essence, there is much to be gained from the stories of Julio Ramón Ribeyro.

Translator's Note

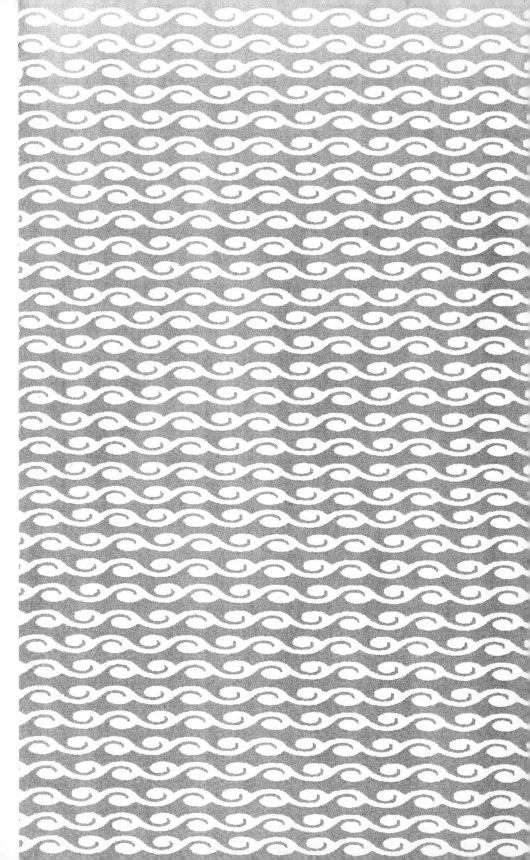

*M*any reasons compel a translator to risk carrying an author's world view across cultural and linguistic borders. This English translation primarily was motivated by my fondness for Julio Ramón Ribeyro's stories and a desire to see a wider circle of readers acquainted with one of Latin America's finest writers of short fiction today. Another motivating factor was the discovery that many of his stories had already made their way into other languages—French, Italian, Portuguese, German, and Chinese to name a few. I was determined that they cross yet another border to reach an English-speaking public.

I cannot give a satisfactory reason why I selected these fifteen stories to translate beyond explaining that crossing borders was foremost on my mind. There are numerous, outstanding examples of Ribeyro's short fiction collected in three volumes originally titled *La palabra del mudo* (Lima, 1972 and 1977) that could just as reasonably be included in this collection. Although the majority of Ribeyro's stories take place in his native Peru, the marginal voices in the texts that appear here are culturally diverse. Together they acquire a universal tone that speaks volumes about the fragile moments in life when illusion and reality collide. True to Ribeyro's canon of works, these stories let us glimpse the solitude and vulnerability that cut across all social, economic, and cultural borders. I believe that the circumstances and settings in which the characters of these stories imaginatively deal with their marginal existence will hold special interest for readers engaged in cross-cultural studies, for students studying English as a second language as well as for those simply reading for pleasure.

I undertook this translation warily, cognizant of the fact that the translation process precludes any exact rendering of the original text. Thanks to Ribeyro's sparse, classical style of writing, unsurmountable challenges did not lurk behind every other word. However, the normal problems associated with literary translation involving word choices, idiomatic expressions, cultural differences, and syntax did surface along the way, demanding thoughtful solutions. I included explanatory notes only when I felt they were needed to identify a word or phrase or to clarify its usage. I can only hope that this translation reflects a very close reading and understanding of Ribeyro's stories and that it approaches the original Spanish as accurately as possible.

The translation of this book has been made possible in part by a Summer Research Grant awarded by Louisiana Tech University.

Special recognition is due to the anthropologist and writer, Dr. José Gushiken of Lima, Peru, who first introduced me to Ribeyro's stories in the early 1970s. His encouragement and willingness to research the usage of several Peruvian words and expressions with respect to their semantic and cultural functions helped to facilitate the always precarious task of literary translation.

I am deeply grateful to my friend and colleague, Jaime Aros, for his editorial help. His meticulous reading of the drafts led to some interesting discussions about varied perspectives of seeing situations. He gave generously of his time and made valuable suggestions.

I want to thank Professor Robert E. Jungman and Tom J. Lewis for their advice and help with the manuscript and C. V. Douglas for proofreading.

I would like to recognize *Fiction Network*, where my translation of the story "El profesor suplente" ("The Substitute Teacher") first appeared in English in issue 8, 1988, and the publishers of Intercultural Press, who published the first English translation of "Alienation" in 1986.

Finally, I want to express my gratitude to Julio Ramón Ribeyro for responding to my inquiries about his fiction long before the project became a reality, to the University of Texas Press for supporting this endeavor, and to Theresa J. May for her perseverance from start to finish.

DIANNE DOUGLAS

Marginal Voices

Terra Incognita

*D*octor Alvaro Peñaflor interrupted his reading of Plato's work that he held in his hands and stared out the large windows of his library, contemplating the lights of Lima which extended from La Punta to Morro Solar. It was an unusually clear wintry evening. He could make out luminous signs blinking on tall buildings and behind them the dark contour of the ocean and the outline of San Lorenzo Island.

When he tried to resume his reading he noticed he was distracted, that from the vast galaxy at his feet, a voice was calling him. Accustomed to exact analyses, he again examined the window and searched himself, finally discovering that the voice was not coming from outside, but rather from inside himself. That voice was telling him: Go out, get to know your city, live.

Days earlier the voice had tried to make its presence known, but he had stifled it. His wife and two daughters had left for the United States and Mexico on an economy tour two weeks earlier, and since then, for the first time since he married, he was completely alone. After twenty years of saving, he had built that house on a hill in the Monterrico section and now he was alone in it, in the place where he believed he had found the ideal refuge for a man indifferent to worldly ambitions, dedicated solely to the pleasures of the intellect.

But solitude has many faces. He had only known literary solitude, the kind that poets and philosophers talked about, and on which he had given seminars at the university and even written a fine article praised by his colleague Doctor Carcopino. However, real solitude is another thing. Now that he was living it, he realized how space and time grew and expanded when a person found himself on his own, abandoned in a place that, although not big, was becoming impenetrable because there was no voice to respond to his own nor any being who refracted his existence. The maid, old Edelmira, was there, it's true, lost in the interior, busy with mysterious household chores, only the evidence of which he was aware, a waxed floor, laundered shirts, a knock on the door announcing that supper was being served.

The knock came again this time, but the doctor didn't respond. Behind the door Edelmira let out a perplexing exclamation, but when the doctor said for her not to worry because he had a dinner invitation, the sound of some angry footsteps could be heard until they trailed off and faded into silence. Only then did the professor understand that his words had set the stage for his decision, and now, after he had already said it, he had no choice but to put on his coat, look for the car keys, and go downstairs.

As he faced the steering wheel, he found himself completely absorbed in thought. He had a perfectly fine textual knowledge of the old Hellenic cities, the mythological labyrinths, the fortresses where so many heroes perished and gods were wounded, but he knew almost nothing about his native city, aside from the streets he had always taken to get to the university, the national library, Doctor Carcopino's house, or to his mother's home. For that reason, as he drove off, he realized his hands were trembling, that this trip was really an exploration of the unknown, the terra incognita.

He roamed and rambled through new, flourishing urbanized areas whose language he tried in vain to decipher and which told him nothing. Finally a road wrested him away from that archipelago of monotonous, tenebrous comfort and led him to Miraflores, where he seldom went, but a district that held some youthful memories for him: the park, a restaurant with a terrace, passable wine, and girls who then seemed to possess an immortal beauty.

It wasn't difficult for him to locate the place, but he noted that it had been downgraded: the terrace was gone. He took a seat in the noisy interior where friends and relatives were eating pizza and spaghetti. He ordered breaded veal Milanese style and decided to have a Chilean wine. A quick survey of his surroundings was enough to make him realize that it was useless to get his hopes up. The bucolic beauties of his adolescence had disappeared, were probably frequenting other places or were now satiated, imposing matrons reigning over a table, brandishing a fork as a symbol of their regal power.

Nevertheless, after finishing his wine, he noticed the place had become more cheerful. He even noticed a woman alone, beautiful besides, who was indecisively observing a pyramid of ice cream with whipped cream, cherries, and chocolate, seemingly unsure about how she should attack it. Forgetting everyone else, he focused his attention only on her. She had Medusa's curly hair and a profile that he classed as Alexandrian. He amused himself by inventing careers for her—psychologist, poet, stage actress—until their eyes met. That happened several times and the professor began to find the night diabolically seductive. He ordered a half bottle more of wine, lighted a cigarette, studied the establishment's decor for a moment; when he turned to look at the woman again, he was surprised to find that she had devoured her ice cream in the twinkling of an eye, called the waiter, paid her bill, and was leaving. From this moment on, the place became gloomy. The professor strained to savor his wine, anxiously searching for the voice that was calling him earlier, not hearing anything from within or without. This night out had been a total disaster. There was nothing for him but to return to his reading of Plato.

But on the street the cool air revived him; he listened to the sound of the ocean and instead of taking the route home he drove down the main avenue, looking at the sidewalks where late shoppers were drifting, new cafes closing, and trees swaying in the limpid night, until he came to little Salazar Park. To his surprise groups of boys and girls were still strolling along the walks or chatting around a bench. There weren't many, but they were there and it was comforting to see them because they symbolized something—they were like night militiamen refusing to abandon a city being overcome by sleep.

He parked his car and watched them for awhile. The young people circling counterclockwise would stop when they came upon each other, converse for a moment, and resume their walk, some of them exchanging places. Those standing around the bench would surrender a few of their members to the strollers and receive others in exchange. It seemed like chaotic comings and goings, but in reality they were rigorously obeying rules established long ago. Thus, the beginnings of the Athenian city-state must have emerged in small spaces like this, where people gathered, got acquainted, talked, and confronted each other.

One figure among the rest intrigued him. It was a long-haired girl in pants who seemed to represent an extreme position in a debate because she was being accosted by everyone and was defending herself by making comical, mocking moves or gesturing so as to keep her adversaries at a distance. Suddenly something happened because the ones near the bench kept quiet and the strollers imitated them; everyone was motionless, looking in his direction, the only parked car there at that hour. From a distance they gave the impression that they were having a discussion in a low voice; an envoy, the girl with the long hair, left the group to investigate. As she was approaching, the professor studied her features and her shape, but when she was near the car, he discovered that it was really a boy. The adolescent passed by the car door, giving him impudent looks, and ran back to his friends. He said something to them because they laughed. Some pointed a finger at him, another made an ambiguous gesture with his arm. He clearly heard the word "old man" and others that he halfway understood but that left him confused. The age-old agora dispersed; it was contaminated. Starting the car, he drove away in shame.

He drove distractedly, straying through gloomy, tree-lined streets with no one in sight, and even if there had been he wouldn't have noticed because in spirit he was in his library with seven thousand volumes surrounding him as he traveled through reigns, wars, coronations, and disasters on the arm of Xenophon or Thucydides. He hated having yielded to that banal temptation, that excursion through the outer limits of serenity, forgetting that years ago he had chosen a lifestyle of reading old manuals, of patiently translating Homeric texts and of nurturing the illusive, yet stubborn goal of creating an ancient image of worldly life, probably skeptical, but harmonious and bearable.

The sound of a horn belonging to a van about to hit him jolted him from his thoughts. He had just crossed a bridge spanning the expressway, the astringent wine had made his throat dry, that lively neighborhood had to be Surquillo, he noticed the bright sign of a bar. El Triunfo, they said, was a den of drunks and brawls, it couldn't be the sound of the ocean that he was hearing but rather the singing of sirens, his books were so far away and his throat was burning with thirst, his car had already stopped in front of the place and he was boldly walking toward the swinging door.

Instead of sirens, hairy, grim men were having beers at cubicles along the wall or at small tables in the center of the room. He sat down at one of the tables in the middle, ordered a beer, and relished the bitter coolness of his first sip, repeated it, filling his mouth with the froth. Nights could be eternal if one knew how to use them. He entertained himself by looking at the way the liquor shelves caved in under the weight of all the bottles, but when he really tried to give meaning and order to his surroundings, he realized that nothing made sense; the place said nothing to him and he had nothing to say to it. He was lost, thirsting in the desert, the terrified castaway searching in the fog for the shore of the island of Circe. Citrine figures in white jackets glided over the tile with plates in their hands; a fat siren appeared at one of the side cubicles, closely pursued by a legion of young studs; in another area someone was drying glasses with a dirty rag, someone was making notes Chinese-style in a bank book, someone was laughing at his side and when he looked at him he saw a face on which had been etched for millions of years the features of the saurian tyrant; he put another glass to his lips, looking for the answer in the froth, and now the siren was a Venus Hotentote harassed by the horseflies, happy satyrs heading for a dark door with their hands on the fly of their pants, and the place was filled with flies, heavy vapors, and bellows. When he raised his arm, he had at his neck a greasy bow tie. He put out a few bills and left, scrupulously looking at his shoes as he put one foot in front of the other, moving forward over the geometrical figures he couldn't make out on the floor, among cigarette butts and bottle caps.

He tottered along the sidewalk, his car had to be here somewhere; he advanced about a hundred meters, made it to the corner and another bar was opening its enormous doors to him; small marble tables held a shrill bunch of people who were making reckless gestures with their arms. He didn't feel like going in, so he continued on his way, still searching, but it wasn't the right way, the asphalt had disappeared, street lamps became scarce, dogs swiftly crossed his path, he heard water running in a ditch smelling of heath, a winged creature grazed his head. He was in the realm of shadows. The place where the vanquished gods must be buried, the murdered heroes of the *Iliad*.

A narrow passage absorbed him and he found himself with his elbows propped on a wooden counter. The sounds of frogs croaking could be heard in the distance. Behind those adobe walls must be the open fields. He thought he had read a sign painted with a stubby brush at the entrance that said El Botellón.[1] That's why he ordered a *botellón* and the *botellón* was there, spewing foam from its mouth, and he couldn't resist grabbing it between his hands, that's what he wanted, the rules had been broken, he lifted it with a gesture of adoration and drank from the bottle like the others, while he listened to a man who was talking at his side or reciting or singing, he didn't know which, he had a stained face, and from his thick lips came a rhythmic discourse, esteemed sir, your humble servant, taking advantage of the circumstances, son of a sugarcane worker, it's never too late to learn, to tell you in all modesty . . .

What was he saying? He struggled to focus his attention and discovered the giant, the invincible warrior resting from his battles and amusing himself by telling stories of his deeds. The counter was supporting his rough hand bearing battle scars. But upon closer inspection, he wasn't a warrior, he was a civil hero confessing his guilt before being executed. No, he wasn't even that, but just a corpulent, black man, half-drunk, who was toasting him with his bottle and asking him for a cigarette.

The professor offered him one and was immediately rewarded with a slap on the back. But, after drinking a foaming bottle, now he was listen-

1. The Spanish word *botellón* refers to a big bottle of alcoholic beverage.

ing to him, eleven brothers and sisters, his truck needed a tire, Don Belisario was a son of a bitch, if you'll pardon my French, and all this history so full of rewards, refrains, and parentheses, fascinating him like the reading of a hermetic text and in turn he bought him a bottle while excitedly injecting a comment that made his interlocutor reflective and forced new comments from him, and in no time at all he was the one who was talking; for some strange reason he turned to poetry and the eyes of the giant opened wide; from his swollen lips flowed a ballad in response to a quote from Anacreon,[2] but everything was so fragile, the tight thread was about to snap; behind the counter someone was shouting that everyone had to leave, just when the black man was laughing and putting his hand on his shoulder, it's already three in the morning, we don't have a permit, the sound of pounding on the counter and they all got to their feet, the door was closing and they kept going out into the dark street in groups, couples locked in embraces were taking secret paths to toast the dawn and the black man was asking him, distinguished sir, where, dear friend, are we going to have our last bottle and he answered at my house.

Something had happened. The black man brusquely leaned against him as they rounded a curve; he lost control of the helm and they smashed into a clay fence: a dent on the fender. But that was now ancient history, as distant as the Battle of Thermopylae. They had entered the library and the black man almost fell backward when he saw all the books; he asked whether he had read all of them and ended up sinking down into a leather easy chair, the same one in which Doctor Carcopino, for so many years, would sprawl as he told him of his recent readings in Roman history. But this wasn't the most important thing, nor was the accident, nor the stranger there in Carcopino's place; it was something else, the thread had snapped or become entangled, the professor was seated before the colossus and he saw his enormous eyes looking at him and his heavy hands motionless on the chair's armrests, not saying or asking for anything, as if he were outside of time, spying on him, waiting. Then, of course, he remembered, they had come for a drink and now he was asking himself where he would find something to offer a toast, since there was never anything to drink in the house, so he excused himself and went to sniff out the dining room, the kitchen, but quietly so Edelmira

2. Anacreon was a Greek poet who wrote of wine, women, and the pleasures of love.

wouldn't be awakened, old women were light sleepers and his hands trembled in the darkness, groping at glasses, salad bowls, until he decided to turn on the light and discovered a store of forgotten bottles, a *pisco*,[3] whiskey, a port, all which he carried to the library on a tray with a little ice. The black man's eyes beamed and his lips smiled, but he didn't say anything, so he had to ask him what he wanted, a *pisco*, naturally, in another goblet he poured whiskey and when he made the first toast it was as though they were at the Botellón again; the giant was talking about his eleven brothers and sisters, the son of a bitch Don Belisario, pardon my French, and the doctor felt the urge to kill off that tyrannical master and at the same time to tear into the hard, sweet sugarcane with his teeth and to walk barefoot on the southern beaches.

During the second toast, he took over and began expounding on agriculture during the time of Pericles and his words flowed as if from a golden urn, all the flowers of his erudition spontaneously budding, and without a pause he turned from cultivation to sculpture, delighting in his own eloquence at that late hour, almost overwhelmed by the splendor of an intelligence sparkling before an interlocutor who gave no sign of life other than an open mouth getting wider by the minute, and since he was perspiring, he unfastened some of the buttons on his shirt, exposing a curved thorax of masculine magnificence. Then the professor realized he had not been mistaken, that in the Botellón he had seen correctly, that man was the archaic hero, the image of Aristogiton,[4] and he told him so, but since he didn't interpret the message, he ended up pouring himself another drink, stood up to inspect his library books, forgetting about everything else except exactly where that book was and opening it he showed him the splendorous figure of a nude man with his armed raised in a triumphant gesture.

The black man looked at it a long time, without showing much interest, and ended up saying, naked, his thing is dead and by breaking into laughter, while he was unfastening another button on his shirt revealing a scapulary of Jesus the Miracle Worker. The professor was already telling the story about that Athenian citizen who together with a friend assassinated a despot and was tortured to death for it, but he abruptly stopped when he saw the scapulary. Then he closed his book, vacillating, but now it was the black man who was saying distinguished professor,

3. *Pisco* is an alcoholic drink that originated in Pisco, Peru. It is derived from wine and other substances and is usually diluted with water.
4. Aristogiton was an Athenian patriot who, along with his homosexual lover Harmodius, slew Hipparchus, tyrant of Athens.

faith is inherited, dear doctor, I have carried the sacred litter three times, listen friend, religion is one thing and life another, you know, that doesn't stop you from forgetting your physical needs and now he was serving himself another drink while pointing to the closed book that the doctor was holding against his chest and he repeated the comment about the naked man whose thing is dead and broke into an even bigger fit of laughter stamping his feet against the carpeted floor. The professor was just about to imitate him but he collected himself, went toward the shelves to put up his book, thinking about the abyss that separates cultures, of writing an essay on the way to make art accessible to the masses; he placed the book where it belonged, perhaps show him other pictures, but when he turned his head he noticed that the black man was holding his empty glass in his hand and that he had fallen asleep in the easy chair, completely shirtless and covered with sweat. Then he looked toward the windows and saw the lights of Lima still crying out anxiously in the fearless night.

He took off his coat and sat down in a chair; not knowing what to do, he poured himself another whiskey. On his desk he spotted a stack of papers, a course he was preparing on Aristophanes, but he forgot all that and turned to look at the sleeping giant, an illusive Aristogiton who was slowly beginning to take on the look of a drunk truck driver. For a moment he imagined Doctor Carcopino coming in with a bundle of papers under his arm, but indignantly rejected this image, and again looked through the windows; lighted signs were being turned off, somehow signaling the approaching dawn. Edelmira was an early riser and the first thing she did when she got up was collect the dirty ashtrays and coffee cups from the library. He approached the easy chair and brushed his hand against the colossus' cheek, but was only able to extract a snore from him. With both hands he slapped him, harder and harder, letting his head bounce from side to side, but with no response; the glass slipped from his hand. He went into the bathroom and came out with a wet towel that he rubbed against his forehead, face, and shoulders, but nothing phased this heavy monolith. Finally he grabbed him by his wrists and tried to lift him, an unequal match, but he was able to draw close for an instant, before giving way under his weight; he managed to separate him from the back of the chair and stand him almost upright only to fall on top of him then, in an embrace, smelling his sweat, feeling the skin of his chest against his face and his poorly shaven chin as it scraped his forehead; he found his throat and squeezed it; his enormous eyes opened wide, frightened eyes, what the hell, he pushed him backward, he was just about to fall, but he must have remembered something because now he was apologizing, distinguished sir, anyone can fall asleep, illustrious professor, his eyes blinking as he looked at his bare chest, his shirt on the floor and then the professor in turn asking him to pardon him, nothing has happened, I'll call a taxi and the black man looked down at his own torso, his trousers, and let himself fall in the easy chair inquiring about his drink, I need another one, listen here, but that isn't possible, there's the shower, a stream of cold water will fix you up and at last Aristogiton was on his feet, more robust than ever, asking why he had to leave and if there wasn't a bed that he could flop into.

The sound of water was coming from the shower while dawn was breaking. The professor was in his easy chair, smoking, exhaustively looking at the seven thousand books surrounding him. The taxi had to be on its way. Maybe in the guest room, if only he had thought about it sooner, to abandon someone that way. A thundering voice came from the bathroom, and with a start the professor stood up, Edelmira being a light sleeper, Doctor Carcopino, he was asking for a towel and dared to make a joke about the water spouts being so fat and curved and he had to go in with a huge towel and see the vigorous, dark form against the white majolica background while the colossus still halfway lost between the Botellón, the land, the shower, and the scapulary kept saying that religion has nothing to do with life's needs and that after all why worry, there would always be a soft bed to fall into and something that would let him change the tire on his truck.

The professor had grown quiet. He forgot about the guest room, he had heard the sound of a car horn below, he still didn't know the black man's sense of timing, the taxi driver would ring the doorbell, some people took longer than others to dress, but the black man was one of the quick ones; now he was in the library buttoning his shirt, still smiling, a drink sure would hit the spot, then some hot coffee. The sky was already light, he could take a bottle with him but he couldn't have any coffee, he had to understand, his duties, and he was pushing him toward the stairs, the black man offering little resistance, these things happened, distinguished professor, it's been a pleasure, but someone has to pay the taxi, you know. I'm always at your service, every night at the Botellón, and the bill passed from one hand to the other and finally the door was closed and locked and the professor, panting, could go back up to his library.

He looked out the windows. The taxi was driving away in an already vanished city. Papers were still stacked high on his desk, all his books in the bookshelves, his family abroad, and within him an image of himself. But it was no longer the same.

PARIS, AUGUST 1975

Barbara

*F*or ten years I kept Barbara's letter. For a while I carried it in my pocket in hopes of finding someone who would translate it for me. Then I stashed it away in a satchel along with other old papers. Finally, one afternoon, seized by one of those sudden surges of reckless energy when one takes frenzied delight in annihilating all traces of the past, I tore it up along with whatever else one tears up on those occasions: used train tickets from some long trip, receipts from a hotel where we were happy, programs from some forgotten play. Thus, there was nothing left to remind me of Barbara and I'll never know what it was she wanted to tell me in that letter written in Polish.

It happened in Warsaw, years after the end of the war. From the ruins the Poles had built a new capital, rather ugly, crammed with concrete buildings that an architect would probably classify as a product of totalitarianism. I was one of thirty thousand boys who attended one of those Youth Congresses which eventually were phased out. We were optimists and full of hope then. We believed that all we had to do was to bring together young people from different parts of the world and have them spend fifteen days with one another in a big city taking excursions, talking, dancing, eating, and drinking in order to create peace on earth. We knew nothing about mankind or history.

I saw her at one of the friendship visits—get-togethers they were called—that the Polish young people would give for the foreign delegates. Her head was perfectly round and golden and she was petite, agile, refined, and with a profile so delicate that one was almost afraid to stare at it for fear it might shatter. Through gestures we became friends. At the get-togethers, which gave us a chance for cultural exchange and to show off our talents, one of us danced and Barbara sang a mystifying, countrified song that totally captivated us.

She worked in a laboratory where I went looking for her several times. On Lenin Plaza, in front of the Cultural Palace, we gathered with all the other thousands of young people in the evenings and danced to the mingled rhythms of several orchestras. Afterward, everyone would go to a dark park not far away where, in the name of universal solidarity, we kissed. The first time I squeezed her with such brutality that she folded, weak and breathless in my arms.

Unlike the other boys who quickly made lovers of their friends—in the evenings, back in our rooms, they would light up cigarettes and tell stories of despicable and violent moments of fornication—my relationship with Barbara was ambiguous and measured. This was mostly because we couldn't understand one another. Barbara spoke Polish and Russian, and I, Spanish and French. Forced to use gestures and signals, our friendship was limited more so by the absence of true love that conquers all. There was only lust on my part, but lust that I could only act upon first through verbal communication, in this case impossible.

One night while we were having a beer, an abominable liquid in a bar that pretended to be Western, I noticed that Barbara wanted to tell me something. On other occasions I had seen her make the same gesture, but now she was more explicit: she grabbed her skirt, caressed the material and pulled the hem of her skirt toward her knees or lifted it carelessly, exposing part of her exquisite thigh. What did Barbara want? Could it be that finally she understood what I wanted? I laughed to see her so vulnerable and willing to reveal to me her innermost thoughts. It took a flurry of gesturing before I understood that what she wanted to tell me was this: I live on the outskirts of the city; we will go to my house one day; we have to go by train.

At last the beautiful Barbara had yielded and she understood! I too would be able to go back to the dorm, light up a cigarette, and tell my story about the virile Latin who collected his share in the flower garden of Central Europe; it would be something to laugh about, to remember later and boast about, until life managed to diminish its significance and reduce it to a petty incident.

The trip finally came about one hot afternoon. It had been postponed several times, I supposed because of some obstacle that kept us from being alone in the house. All the strategy for this pastoral tryst I left up to Barbara, afraid that the Congress would end without us reaching our common goal.

But that hot afternoon she made me understand that the moment had come, and we walked far away from Lenin Square, to the train station. There were only three train cars, all packed with working-class people, that made the daily run between one of Warsaw's parks and the suburbs to the south. Climbing aboard, I realized that I was probably the only foreigner who dared to break away from the more-or-less official schedule to which we were confined. Hence, the trip became more than a romantic rendezvous; it was a forbidden act.

The train crossed the suburbs, then the planted fields, and within twenty minutes it stopped in a little town where Barbara had me get off. In one of the large rooms at the station we acquired two bicycles that were public property used by the local residents; thus we continued our trip that from then on began to take on for me a tinge of the unreal. We followed dirt paths banked by walls and trees; we passed by old manors graced with vegetable and flower gardens, we came across farmers who watched as we passed by, we startled rural dogs who jumped up barking at us from behind fences, and as we speeded up Barbara was still in front of me, energetically pedaling; I behind her, fascinated by her round head and golden ponytail.

She finally stopped in front of a rather small house with a wooden fence facing the street. I followed her lead and together, laughing, happy, perspiring, we pushed our bicycles past the gate, into the garden. Barbara reached for my hand, and we ran up the wooden steps leading to the front door. She took a key from her purse and threw open the door. We stepped inside a dark vestibule and then entered a living room that I quickly inspected—old, rustic furniture—searching for a sofa where we might rest a moment, setting the mood, communicating somehow, now that words didn't matter; my hands would be eloquent, and I felt so sure of myself that I couldn't have cared less about the man with the broad mustache who was observing me from a carved wooden frame, Barbara saying bang-bang, chopping away at her leg with her hand, then sounding tac-tac-tac-tac, explaining to me that he was her father, an invalid from the war, a railroad employee.

But we didn't stay in the living room for long. Barbara was in such a hurry, she couldn't sit still; she dragged me by the hand along a hallway, pushed open another door, and we found ourselves in a bedroom where the first thing I saw was a rather narrow bed covered with a flowered, cotton quilt. A bed. What a long journey it had been from our first meeting to this small space, as sparse as a tomb, but so adequate, where at last our bodies would speak the same language.

Barbara took off her dress and moved toward the bed; but instead of lying down she circled it and hurried toward an enormous closet, chattering in Polish, without worrying whether or not I understood her. Suddenly she flung open the closet doors.

I saw half a dozen skirts suspended from hangers. Barbara took them out and tried them on one by one, pointing out their printed designs, inviting me to feel the material, explaining the cut, function, and style of each one in her baffling language, which I was hearing but not really comprehending. Finally, without taking off the last skirt, she became subdued and silent as she faced the pile of clothing on the bed, her eager eyes intently fixed on me.

"Many skirts," I said finally.

But she seemed to be waiting for something more and continued interrogating me with her eyes.

"Pretty skirts," I added. "*Lindas, molto bellas,* beautiful, many skirts, pretty skirts."

She had understood and smiled. Sighing, she paused for a moment, observing the articles of clothing, and then, slowly, she began putting them back on their hangers and returned them to the closet. She took out a blouse and put it on. After closing the wardrobe doors she smiled, indicating that we should leave. We didn't linger in the living room this time either—another quick glance and the man with the mustache seemed to me sullen, ferocious—and soon we found ourselves once again in the garden reaching for our bicycles. I felt stunned, stupid; I followed her like a dummy; I mounted my bike, and there I was again pedaling down the path lined with flowers, trailing behind the round head and the blazing ponytail, en route to the train station.

We left our bicycles in the same depository and minutes later we were taking the suburban train back to Warsaw. Barbara didn't say a word, but I detected neither hostility nor regret but something more like relief, contentment, and peace of mind. She smiled every time she looked at me as if I were her most intimate friend, the one who shared her secrets and who had been given the privilege of contemplating more than her nakedness, her possessions.

The following day we left for our return trip to Paris. The railway cars were jammed full of boys drinking, singing, and saying their final goodbyes to their transitory lovers through the windows. In vain I looked for Barbara among the people on the platform.

It was months later that I received her letter.

PARIS, 1972

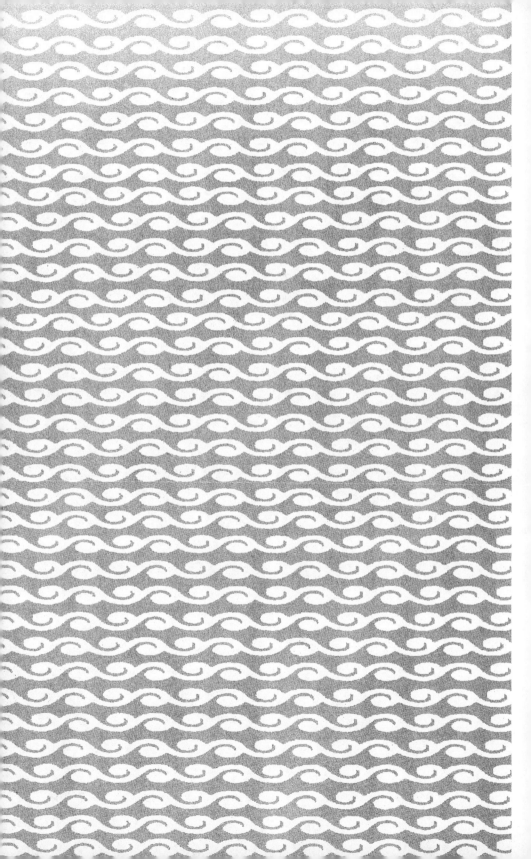

The Featherless Buzzards

*A*t six in the morning the city gets up on tiptoe and slowly begins to stir. A fine mist dissolves the contour of objects and creates an atmosphere of enchantment. People walking about the city at this hour seem to be made of another substance, to belong to a ghostly order of life. Devout women humbly shuffle along, finally disappearing in the doorways of churches. The night-wanderers, drubbed by the darkness, return home wrapped up in mufflers and melancholy. Garbage collectors begin their sinister stroll down Pardo Avenue, armed with brooms and carts. There are workers heading for the streetcars, policemen yawning next to trees, newspaper boys turning purple from the cold, and maids putting out trash cans. Finally, at this hour, as if responding to some mysterious password, the featherless buzzards appear.

At this hour old Don Santos fastens on his wooden leg, sits down on the mattress, and starts to bellow, "Efraín, Enrique! Get up! Now!"

The two boys run to the ditch inside the corral,[1] rubbing their bleary eyes. The calm night has settled the water, making it transparent to reveal growing weeds and agile infusories sliding about. After washing their faces, each boy grabs his can and scurries toward the street. Meanwhile, Don Santos goes to the pigpen and whacks the pig on the back with his long stick as the animal wallows in filth.

"You still have a way to go, you dirty rascal! Just you wait; your time's coming."

Efraín and Enrique are lingering in the street, climbing trees to snatch berries or picking up stones, the tapered kind that cut through the air and sting the back. Still enjoying the celestial hour, they reach their domain, a long street lined with elegant houses leading to the levee.

They aren't alone. In other corrals and in other suburbs someone has given a sound of alarm and many have gotten up. Some carry tin cans, others cardboard boxes, and sometimes just an old newspaper is enough. Unaware of each other, together they form a kind of clandestine organization that works the city. There are those who maraud through public buildings, others choose the parks or the dunghills. Even the dogs have acquired certain habits and schedules, wisely coached by poverty.

1. Corral here refers to an enclosed, dirt yard surrounding the one-room shack in the urban slums of Peru, where Efraín, Enrique, and their grandfather live.

After Efraín and Enrique take a short rest, they begin their work. Each one chooses a side of the street. Garbage cans are lined up in front of the doors. They have to be completely emptied before the exploration begins. A garbage can is always like a box full of surprises. There are sardine cans, old shoes, pieces of bread, dead parakeets, and soiled cotton balls. The boys, however, are only interested in scraps of food. Although Pascual will eat anything thrown to him in his pen, his favorite food is partially decomposed vegetables. Each goes along filling up his small can with rotten tomatos, pieces of fat, exotic salsas that never show up in cookbooks. It's not unusual, however, to make a real find. One day Efraín found some suspenders that he made into a slingshot. Another time he discovered an almost eatable pear that he devoured on the spot. Enrique, on the other hand, has a knack for finding small medicine boxes, brightly colored bottles, used toothbrushes, and similar things that he eagerly collects.

When they have rigorously sorted through everything, they dump the garbage back in the can and head for the next one. It doesn't pay to take too long because the enemy is always lying in wait. Sometimes the maids catch them off guard and they have to flee, scattering their spoils behind them. But more often than not the sanitation department cart sneaks up on them and then the whole workday is lost.

When the sun peeks over the hills, the celestial hour comes to an end. The mist lifts, the devout women are immersed in ecstasy, the night nomads are asleep, the paper boys have delivered their papers, and the workers have mounted the platforms. Sunlight fades the magical world of dawn. The featherless buzzards have returned to their nest.

Don Santos had made coffee and was waiting for them.

"Let's have it. What did you bring me today?"

He would sniff among the cans and if the grub was good he always made the same remark: "Pascual's going to have a feast today."

But most of the time he blurted out, "You idiots! What did you do today? You must have just played around! Pascual's going to starve to death!"

The boys would run for the grape arbor, their ears still burning from the slaps, while the old man dragged himself over to the pigpen. From the far end of his fort the pig would start to grunt while Don Santos tossed him scraps of food.

"My poor Pascual! You'll stay hungry today because of those loafers.

They don't spoil you like I do. I'll have to give them a good beating and teach them a lesson."

At the beginning of winter the pig had turned into an insatiable monster. He couldn't get enough to eat and Don Santos took out the animal's hunger on his grandsons. He made them get up earlier to search unfamiliar areas for more scraps. Finally he forced them to go as far as the garbage dump along the ocean's edge.

"You'll find more stuff there. It'll be easier, too, because everything will be together."

One Sunday Efraín and Enrique reached the edge. The sanitation department carts were following tracks on a dirt road, unloading trash on a rocky slope. Viewed from the levee, the dump formed a dark, smoky bluff of sorts where buzzards and dogs gathered like ants. From a distance the boys threw stones to scare off their competition. A dog backed off yelping. When the boys reached the dump, they were overcome by a nauseating smell that seeped into their lungs. Their feet sank into a pile of feathers, excrement, and decayed or charred matter. Burying their hands in it, they began their search. Sometimes they would discover a half-eaten carrion under a yellowed newspaper. On the nearby bluffs the buzzards impatiently spied on them; some approached, jumping from one rock to another as though they were trying to corner the boys. Efraín tried to intimidate them by shouting; and his cries echoed in the gorge, shaking loose some large pebbles that rolled toward the sea. After working for an hour they returned to the corral with their cans filled.

"Bravo!" Don Santos exclaimed. "We'll have to do this two or three times a week."

From then on, Efraín and Enrique made their trek to the sea on Wednesdays and Sundays. Soon they became part of the strange fauna of those places and the buzzards, accustomed to their presence, worked at their side, cawing, flapping their wings, scarping with their yellow beaks as if helping them to uncover the layer of precious filth.

One day when Efraín came back from one of his excursions, he felt a sore on the bottom of his foot. A piece of glass had made a small wound. The next day his foot was swollen, but he continued his work. By the time they returned he could hardly walk, but Don Santos was with a visitor and didn't notice him. He was observing the pigpen, accompanied by a fat man with blood-stained hands.

"In twenty or thirty days I'll come back," the man said. "By then I think he'll be just about ready."

When he left, sparks shot from Don Santos' eyes.

"Get to work! Get to work! From now on we've got to see that Pascual gets more to eat! We're going to pull this deal off."

The next morning, however, when Don Santos woke his grandsons, Efraín couldn't get up.

"His foot's sore," Enrique explained. "He cut himself on a piece of glass yesterday."

Don Santos examined his grandson's foot. Infection had set in.

"Nonsense! Have him wash his foot in the ditch and wrap a rag around it."

"But it's really hurting him!" Enrique added. "He can't walk right."

Don Santos thought a moment. Pascual could be heard still grunting in his pen.

"And what about me?" he asked, slapping his wooden leg. "You think my leg doesn't hurt? I'm seventy years old and I work . . . so just stop your whining!"

Efraín left for the street with his can, leaning on his brother's shoulder. Half an hour later they returned with their cans almost empty.

"He couldn't go on!" Enrique told his grandpa. "Efraín's half-crippled."

Don Santos looked at his grandsons as if he were passing sentence on them.

"Okay, okay," he said scratching his thin beard and grabbing Efraín by the scruff of the neck he pushed him toward the one-room shack. "The sick go to bed! Lay there and rot! Enrique, you'll do your brother's work. Get out of here! Go to the dump!"

Around noon Enrique came back with both cans filled. A strange visitor was following him: a squalid, mangy dog. "I found him at the dump," Enrique explained, "and he kept following me."

Don Santos picked up the stick. "One more mouth to feed!"

Enrique grabbed the dog and, clutching him close to his chest, ran toward the door. "Don't you hurt him, Grandpa! I'll give him some of my food."

Don Santos walked toward him, his wooden leg sinking into the mud. "No dogs here! I already have enough trouble with you boys!"

Enrique opened the door leading to the street. "If he goes, I go, too."

The grandfather paused. Enrique took advantage of the moment and persisted: "He hardly eats anything; look how skinny he is. Besides, since

Efraín's sick, he'll be a help to me. He knows the dump real well and he's got a good nose for scraps."

Don Santos looked up at the dreary sky, gray with drizzle, and thought a moment. Without a word he threw down the stick, picked up the cans, and limped off toward the pigsty.

Enrique smiled with delight and clasping his friend to his heart, he ran to see his brother.

"Pascual, Pascual . . . Pascualito!" the grandfather was chanting.

"We'll name you Pedro," Enrique said, petting the dog's head as he went in the room where Efraín was lying.

His joy suddenly vanished when he saw Efraín writhing in pain on the mattress and drenched in sweat. His swollen foot looked as though it was made of rubber and pumped with air. His toes had almost lost their shape.

"I brought you this present, look," he said, showing him the dog. "His name's Pedro; he's yours, to keep you company. When I go to the dump I'll leave him with you and you can play all day long. You can probably teach him to fetch rocks for you."

"What about Grandpa?" Efraín asked, stretching his hand toward the dog.

"Grandpa has nothing to say about it," Enrique sighed.

They both looked toward the door. The drizzle had begun to fall and they could hear their grandfather's voice calling, "Pascual, Pascual . . . Pascualito!"

That same night there was a full moon. The boys felt uneasy because that was when their grandfather became unbearable. Since late afternoon they had seen him roaming about the corral, talking to himself, swinging away at the grape arbor with his stick. Now and then he would come near the room, scan the interior, and seeing that his grandsons were silent, he would spit on the floor with rage. Pedro was scared of him and every time he saw him he would huddle up and not move a muscle.

"Trash, nothing but trash!" the old man kept repeating all night long as he looked at the moon.

The next morning Enrique woke up with chills. Although the old man had heard him sneeze earlier that morning, he said nothing. Deep down, however, he could sense disaster. If Enrique was sick, what would become of Pascual? The pig's appetite grew more voracious as he got fatter. In the afternoons he would bury his snout in mud and grunt. Nemesio had even come over from his corral a block away to complain.

On the second day the inevitable happened: Enrique couldn't get up. He had coughed throughout the night and by morning he was shivering, burning with fever.

"You, too?" the grandfather asked.

Enrique pointed to his congested, croupy chest. The grandfather stormed out of the room. Five minutes later he returned.

"It's mean to trick me this way!" he whined. "You abuse me because I can't walk. You know damn well that I'm old and crippled. If I could I'd send you both to hell and I'd see to Pascual myself!"

Efraín woke up whimpering and Enrique began to cough.

"The hell with it! I'll take care of him myself. You're trash, nothing but trash! A couple of pitiful buzzards without feathers! You'll see how I get along. Your grandpa's still tough. But one thing's for sure, no food for you today. You won't get any till you can get up and do your work!"

Through the doorway they saw him unsteadily lift the cans in the air and stumble out to the street. Half an hour later he came back licked. He wasn't as quick as his grandsons and the sanitation department cart had gotten there first. Not only that, the dogs had tried to bite him.

"Filthy trash! I warn you, no food till you work!"

The following day he tried to repeat the whole process, but finally had to give up. His leg with the wooden peg was no longer used to the asphalt pavement and the hard sidewalks; a sharp pain stabbed him in the groin every time he took a step. At the celestial hour on the third day, he collapsed on the mattress with only enough energy to cuss.

"If he starves to death," he shouted, "it'll be your fault!"

That was the beginning of several agonizing, interminable days. The three spent the day cooped up in the room together, silently suffering a kind of forced seclusion. Efraín constantly tossed and turned, Enrique coughed, Pedro got up and after taking a run out in the corral, returned with a rock in his mouth which he deposited in his master's hand. Don Santos, propped up on the mattress, was playing with his wooden leg and hurling ferocious looks at the boys. At noon he dragged himself to the corner of the lot where some vegetables were growing and prepared himself some lunch that he devoured in secret. Occasionally he would toss a piece of lettuce or a raw carrot at his grandsons' bed with the intention of whetting their appetite, and thereby giving his punishment a touch of refinement.

Efraín didn't even have the strength to complain. Enrique was the one who felt invaded by a strange sense of fear because when he looked into his grandfather's eyes, they didn't look familiar. It was as though they had lost their human expression. Every night when the moon came up, he would hold Pedro in his arms and squeeze him so affectionately that he made him whimper. That's when the pig would begin to grunt and the old man wailed as if he were being hanged. Sometimes he would fasten on his wooden leg and go out to the corral. In the moonlight Enrique saw him make ten trips back and forth from the pigpen to the garden, raising his fists and knocking over anything that got in his way. Finally he would come back to the room and glare at them, as if he wanted to blame them for Pascual's hunger.

The last night of the full moon no one could sleep. Pascual's grunts were intolerable. Enrique had heard when pigs are hungry they go crazy like people. The grandfather remained vigilant and didn't even put out the lantern. This time he didn't go out to the corral, nor did he cuss under his breath. Sunk down in his mattress, he stared at the door. A deep-seated anger seemed to be welling up in him and he appeared to be toying with it, making ready to unleash it all at once. When the sky began to lighten over the hills, he opened his mouth, and keeping that dark hole turned toward his grandsons he suddenly bellowed, "Up, up, up!" as he pelted them with blows. "Get up you lazy bums! How long is this going to go on? No more. On your feet!"

Efraín broke into tears. Enrique got up, flattening himself against the wall. He was so mesmerized by the old man's eyes that he felt numb to the pain. He saw the stick come down on his head and for a moment it seemed as though it were made of cardboard instead of wood. Finally he was able to speak. "Not Efraín! It's not his fault! Let me go, I'll go, I'll go to the dump!"

The grandfather stepped back, panting. It took him awhile to catch his breath.

"Right now . . . to the dump . . . take two cans, four cans . . ."

Enrique stepped back, picked up the cans and took off running.

The fatigue from hunger and convalescence made him stumble. When he opened the corral door, Pedro tried to go with him.

"You can't come. Stay here and take care of Efraín."

He took off toward the street, deeply breathing the morning air. On the way he ate some grass and was on the verge of chewing dirt. He was seeing everything through a magical mist. His weakened condition made him light-headed and giddy: he was almost like a bird in flight. At the dump he felt like one more buzzard among many. As soon as the cans were overflowing he started back. The devout, the night-wanderers, the barefoot paper boys, and all the other secretions of early dawn began to scatter over the city. Enrique, once again in his world, contentedly walked among them in his world of dogs and ghosts, bewitched by the celestial hour.

As he came into the corral he felt an overpowering, oppressive air that made him stop in his tracks. It was as if there in the doorway his world ended and another made of mud, grunts, and absurd penitence began. It was surprising, therefore, that this time a calm filled with a sense of doom pervaded the corral, as if all the pent-up violence lay in wait, poised and ready to strike. The grandfather was standing alongside the pigpen, gazing at the far end. He looked like a tree growing out of his wooden leg. Enrique made a noise but the old man didn't move.

"Here are the cans!"

Don Santos turned his back on him and stood still. Enrique, full of curiosity, let go of the cans and ran toward the room. As soon as Efraín saw him, he began to whimper, "Pedro . . . Pedro."

"What's the matter?"

"Pedro bit Grandpa . . . and he grabbed the stick . . . then I heard him yelp."

Enrique left the room. "Pedro, here boy! Pedro, where are you?"

There was no response. The grandfather still didn't move and kept looking at the mud wall. Enrique had a sick feeling. He leaped toward the old man. "Where's Pedro?"

His gaze fell on the pigpen. Pascual was devouring something in the mud. Only the dog's legs and tail were left.

"No!" Enrique shouted, covering his eyes. "No, no!" Through his teary eyes he searched his grandfather's face. The old man avoided him, clumsily turning on his wooden leg. Enrique began to dance around him, pulling at his shirt, screaming, kicking, searching his face for an answer. "Why did you do it? Why?"

The grandfather didn't answer. Finally, his patience snapped and he slapped the boy so hard that he knocked him off his feet. From the ground Enrique observed the old man standing erect like a giant, his eyes fixed on Pascual's feast. Enrique reached for the blood-stained stick, quietly got up and closed in on the old man. "Turn around!" he shouted. "Turn around!"

When Don Santos turned, he saw the stick cutting the air above him, then felt the blow to his cheek.

"Take that!" Enrique screamed in a shrill voice, again raising his hand. Suddenly he stopped, horrified by what he was doing, threw down the stick, and gave the grandfather an almost apologetic look. The old man, holding his face, stepped back on his wooden leg, slipped, and with a loud cry he fell backward into the pigpen.

Enrique took a few steps back. At first he listened closely, but didn't hear a sound. Little by little he again drew near. His grandfather was lying on his back in the muck with his wooden peg broken. His mouth was gaping open and his eyes were searching for Pascual, who had taken refuge in a corner of the pen and was suspiciously sniffing the mud.

Enrique started backing away as stealthily as he had come. His grandfather barely saw him because as Enrique ran toward the room he thought he heard him calling his name with a tone of tenderness in his voice that he had never heard before. "Come back, Enrique, come back! . . ."

"Hurry!" Enrique cried, running up to his brother. "Come on, Efraín! The old man has fallen into the pigpen. Let's get out of here!"

"Where?" Efraín asked.

"Wherever, to the dump, anywhere we can get something to eat, where the buzzards go!"

"I can't stand up!"

Enrique picked up his brother with both hands and pressed him against his chest. They clung to each other so tightly, it almost seemed as if one person was slowly making his way across the corral. When they opened the gate to the street, they realized that the celestial hour had ended and that the city, awake and vigilant, was opening before them its gigantic jaws.

Sounds of a struggle were coming from the pigpen.

PARIS, 1954

Of Modest Color

*T*he first thing Alfredo did when he got to the party was to go straight for the bar. He helped himself to a couple of glasses of rum and then, leaning against a doorframe, he began observing the dance. Almost everybody was paired off with the exception of three or four guys who, like himself, were hovering around the bar or smoking a cigarette on the terrace.

After awhile he began to get bored and asked himself why he had come here. He detested parties, partly because he was a bad dancer, and partly because he didn't know how to talk with girls. Usually the bad dancers would hold their partner's attention with their clever talk that helped detract from the way they were treading on their feet; in turn, the jackasses who didn't know how to chat learned to dance so well that the girls would argue over who got to dance with them. But Alfredo, having none of the qualities of either type but all their defects, was undoubtedly doomed to failure at this kind of gathering.

While he was serving himself a third glass of rum, he caught a glimpse of himself in the mirror at the bar. He looked a little bleary eyed and something in his bland facial expression indicated that the liquor was having its effects. Trying to perk up, he went over to the record player where a group of girls were animatedly choosing songs that they would play later.

"Put on a bolero," he suggested.

The girls looked at him with surprise. They were dealing with an unfamiliar face for sure. Parties in the Miraflores district, despite the fact that they took place weekly in different homes, would bring together the same gang of young men looking for girlfriends. It was those Saturday night dances held in middle-class residences that produced almost all the courtships and marriages in the area.

"We like the mambo better," the boldest girl responded. "The bolero's okay for old people."

Alfredo didn't insist but on his way back to the bar he asked himself if that allusion to old people had anything to do with him. He looked at himself in the mirror again. His skin was still smooth but it was in his eyes where a precocious maturity, the price of voracious reading, seemed to have taken its toll. "Old man's eyes," Alfredo thought disparagingly and poured himself a fourth glass of rum.

Meanwhile, all around him things were coming alive. The party, cold at first, was warming up. Couples were letting go and cutting loose. The influence of the Afro-Cuban music was suppressing the censorship of the timid, hypocritical inhabitants of Lima. Alfredo walked to the terrace and looked toward the street. On the sidewalk one could see greedy eyes, drawn heads, hands clinging to the railing. They belonged to ordinary people excluded from the festivities of life.

A voice came from behind him:"Alfredo!"

When Alfredo turned his head he encountered a small man wearing a silvery tie, who was looking at him with disbelief. "But, what are you doing here, man? An artist like yourself . . ."

"I'm here with my sister."

"It's not right for you to be alone. Come on, I'll introduce you to some girls."

Alfredo let his friend drag him through the dancers to a second room where some girls were seated on a sofa. They shared an obvious affinity that had unified them: they were ugly.

"Here's a friend I'd like for you to meet," he said, and without adding anything else, he abandoned him.

The girls looked at him for a moment and then went on talking. Alfredo felt uncomfortable. He didn't know whether to stay there or leave. He courageously opted for the first but did so awkwardly, without opening his mouth, as if he were an officer of the court in charge of guarding them. They looked up now and then to give him a quick glance, somewhat scared. Alfredo found a way to rescue himself. He took out his pack of cigarettes and offered it to the group. "Smoke?"

The response was dry: "No thanks."

He lit one for himself and after releasing the first puff of smoke, felt more secure. He realized that he would have to take the initiative. "Do you all go to the movies?"

"No."

He ventured yet a third question: "Why don't they open that window? It's very hot."

It was worse this time: he didn't even get a response. From that moment on he kept his mouth shut. The girls, intimidated by his silent presence, got up and went to the other room. Alfredo remained alone in the huge room, feeling perspiration saturating his shirt.

The small man with the silvery tie reappeared. "What? You're still standing here? Don't tell me you haven't danced."

"One dance," Alfredo lied.

"I'm sure you haven't said hello to my sister yet. Come on, she's here with her boyfriend."

They both went into the next room. The birthday girl was dancing a regional waltz with some cadet from the Military School.

"Elsa, Alfredo's here and wants to say hello."

"As soon as this dance is over," Elsa replied without interrupting her quick turns. Alfredo stayed close by, waiting, pondering one of the customary birthday greetings. But Elsa ended that dance and began another and, after that, took the cadet's arm and blithely started walking toward the dining room with a long table filled with hors d'oeuvres.

Forgotten, Alfredo again went to the bar. "I have to dance," he told himself. It was now a matter of moral precedence. While he was having his fifth drink he looked in vain for his sister among the guests. His gaze met that of two grown men who were lustfully watching the girls and immediately he felt assaulted by a flood of lucid and distressful thoughts. What could he, a man twenty-five years old, do at a party for adolescents? He was already past the age of taking shelter "in the shadow of young girls about to blossom." This thought led to others more comforting, and casting a look around him, he tried to find some older girl who wouldn't be intimidated by his manner and intelligence.

Near the entrance hall there were three or four girls looking a little wilted, the kind that have let their best years slip away, obsessed with some impossible, frustrated love, and whose only hope now that they were in their thirties would be a marriage not of love, but of convenience.

Alfredo approached them. His step was rather unsteady, so much so that some of the couples whom he tripped over gave him a furious look. When he reached the group, he was caught by surprise: one of the girls was a former neighbor from his childhood.

"Don't tell me I've changed a lot," Corina said. "You'll make me feel old," and she introduced him to the rest of the group.

Alfredo chatted with them awhile. The five rum drinks were loosening him up enough so he could respond to the tirade of stupid questions. He sensed an atmosphere of interest all about him.

"I suppose you've already finished your studies?" Corina inquired.

"No. I dropped out," Alfredo responded frankly.

"Are you working somewhere?"

"No."

"How lucky!" one of the girls intervened. "You must have a good income, not to work."

Alfredo looked at her: she was a brunette, fairly provocative and sensual. A golden spark of light was greedily shining deep in her green eyes.

"But then, what do you do?" Corina asked.

"I paint."

"But . . . Can you make a living doing that?" the brunette inquired, visibly intrigued.

"I don't know what you call a living," Alfredo said. "I survive, at least."

A silent air of disillusionment was generated all around him. Alfredo thought it was time to ask someone to dance, but they were only playing that damn Afro-Cuban music. He risked extending his hand to the brunette when a bald, elegant man with two white shirt cuffs insolently jutting out of his coatsleeves, invaded the group like a bolt of lightning.

"Now everything's set! Fantastic!" he exclaimed. "Tomorrow we'll go to Chosica with Ernesto and Jorge. The three Puertas sisters will come with us. Isn't it perfect! Carmela and Roxana, too."

There was an explosion of excitement.

"Let me introduce you to a friend of mine," Corina said, motioning to Alfredo.

The bald man shook his hand effusively.

"Great, if you want, you can come with us too. We don't have enough room for Elsa and her cousin. Do you want to bring them in your car?"

Alfredo felt blood rush to his head. "I don't have a car."

The bald man looked at him perplexed, as if he had just heard something absolutely bizarre. A twenty-five-year-old man who didn't have a car in Lima was taken for a real imbecile. The brunette bit her lip and observed his suit and shirt more closely. Then she slowly turned her back on him.

The emptiness began. The bald man had monopolized the group's attention by talking about who would ride with whom, and what the plans for Sunday were.

"We'll have the appetizer in Los Angeles! Then we'll have lunch in Santa María. Won't it be great? Later we will do a little jogging . . ."

Alfredo realized that he was in the way there, too. Little by little he moved away from the group while pretending to be looking at the paintings, tripped over an ashtray, and when he reached the bar, he could still hear the bald man's voice bellowing: "We'll have lunch on the river, great!"

"A rum," he said to a girl behind the counter.

The girl looked at him angrily.

"Didn't you hear me? I want rum."

"Get it yourself. I'm not the maid," she answered and hurried away.

Alfredo filled his glass to the brim. He looked at himself again in the mirror. A lock of hair had fallen over his forehead. His eyes had aged even more. "They are so sunken I can't see them," he muttered. He saw his tight lips: the sign of incipient aggression.

When he got ready to pour himself another, he noticed his sister crossing the room. In a flash he was at her side and had her by the arm.

"Elena, let's dance."

Elena quickly pulled away. "A brother and sister dancing? You're crazy! Besides, you reek of liquor. How many drinks have you had? Go on. Wash your face and rinse out your mouth!"

From that moment on Alfredo wandered from room to room, flagrantly making a spectacle of his solitude. He looked at the garden from the terrace, smoked cigarettes near the record player, had more drinks at the bar, spurned the sympathy of other loners wanting to comment on the ironies of social life, and finally took shelter beneath the stairway, near the door facing the kitchen area. The rum was burning deep inside him.

After the second knock, the door to the work area opened and a maid stuck her head out.

"Give me a glass of water, please."

The maid left the door ajar and went off, performing a few dance steps as she went. Alfredo noticed that inside the kitchen the maids were having their own kind of private party while, at the same time, they prepared the rice with duck.

A slender black girl was singing and swaying with a broom in her arms. Alfredo, without hesitating, pushed the door open and entered the kitchen.

"Let's dance," he told the girl.

The black girl declined as she turned away, laughing, rejecting him with her hand but inciting him with her body. When she was pinned against the wall, she disentangled herself from him. "No! They might see us."

The maid brought the glass of water. "Go ahead and dance," she said. "I'll close the door. Why shouldn't we have a good time too?"

The talking continued until the black girl finally gave in. "Only this one dance," she said.

While the maid was locking the door, Alfredo grasped the girl tightly and began to dance. At that moment he realized he was dancing well, maybe because the alcohol gives a sense of rhythm, when it doesn't take it away, or maybe because his partner was following him with such ease. When that dance ended, they began the next. The black girl accepted the pressure of his body with absolute amenability.

"Do you work here?"

"No, at the house next door. But I've come to help out a little and to look around."

They finished the dance among the casseroles and cooking smells. The rest of the kitchen help kept working, sometimes stopping to look at them, laugh, and make funny remarks.

"Let's turn out the light!"

"What's out there?" Alfredo asked, pointing to the screen door at the back of the kitchen.

"The garden, I think."

"Let's go."

The black girl protested.

"Let's go," Alfredo insisted. "We'll be better off there."

Pushing the door open they found themselves on a veranda overlooking the inner garden. There was a pleasant semidarkness. Alfredo pressed his cheek against the black girl's cheek and danced slowly. The music grew very faint.

"It's strange being here like this, isn't it?" the black girl said. "What will the hosts think!"

"It's not strange," Alfredo said. "You're a woman, aren't you?"

They didn't talk for a long while. Alfredo let himself be carried away by a strange sweetness that hardly had anything to do with sensuality. It was, moreover, a tranquillity of a spiritual nature, born of a recovered sense of self-confidence and of the possibility of having contact with human beings.

Shouting from inside the house was heard. "The cake! They're going to cut the cake!"

Before Alfredo could realize what was happening, the porch lights came on, the garden door opened, and a line of happy couples burst through, linked at the waist, and forming a noisy train, blowing whistles, and shouting at the top of their lungs: "Come on everybody! They're going to cut the cake!"

Alfredo had time to observe something else: they hadn't been alone. At the little tables hidden in the shadows of tree branches some couples had taken refuge and now, also taken by surprise, seemed to be awakening from a dream.

The boisterous train circled the garden several times and then started toward the veranda. When they came upon Alfredo and the black girl, the shouting stopped. There was a brief, stunned silence and the train disbanded toward the interior of the house. Even the couples sunken deep in armchairs got up and the men left, dragging their women away by the hand. Alfredo and the black girl were alone.

"How stupid!" he said smiling. "What's the matter with them?"

"I'm leaving," the black girl said, trying to pull away.

"Stay. We're going to keep on dancing."

He forcefully caught her by the hand. He would have embraced her again if a group of men, among them the owner of the house and the small man with the silvery tie, hadn't appeared at the kitchen door.

"What's going on here?" the owner was saying, shaking his head.

"Alfredo," the little man stammered. "Don't make a fool of yourself."

"Don't you have any respect for the ladies here?" a third gentleman intervened.

"Get out of my house," the owner ordered the black girl. "I don't want to see you around here again. Tomorrow I'm going to speak with your employer."

"She's not going anywhere," Alfredo responded.

"And you leave with her, too, damn it!"

Some woman were poking their heads through the kitchen door. Alfredo thought he recognized his sister who, when she saw him, made a half turn and hurried off.

"Didn't you hear me? Get out of here!"

Alfredo scrutinized the owner of the house and, unable to contain himself, broke into laughter.

"He's drunk," someone said.

When he stopped laughing, Alfredo let go of the black girl's arm.

"Wait for me on Madrid Street"; then he buttoned his coat with dignity, and without so much as a good-bye to anybody, crossed the kitchen, went through the room where the dance had been interrupted, through the garden, and finally out the wooden gate.

"That was very gallant of me," he thought as he went off toward his house, lighting a cigarette. As he came upon his house he stopped: through the open window he could see his father with his back to him, reading a newspaper. As far back as he could remember he had seen his father at the same hour, in the same easy chair, reading the same newspaper. He stayed there for a moment. Then he wet his head under the faucet in the garden and started for Madrid Street.

The black girl was waiting for him. She had taken off her apron and her tight silk dress outlined the simple, decisive lines of her body like those of a wooden totem.

Alfredo took her by the hand and dragged her toward the levee, regretting not having enough money to take her to a movie. He contentedly walked along in silence, with the confidence of a man claiming his woman.

"Why are you doing this?" the black girl asked.

"Come on! It doesn't matter."

"Tomorrow you won't remember a thing."

Alfredo didn't respond. He was again beside his house. Slipping his arm around the feminine shoulders, he leaned on the wall and kept looking through the window where his father was still reading the newspaper. The man must have had a certain intuitiveness because he slowly turned around. When he saw Alfredo and the black girl, he looked perplexed for a second. Then he got up, let the newspaper fall, and yanked the shutters closed.

"Let's go to the levee," Alfredo said.

"Who's that man?"

"I don't know him."

That part of the levee was dark. There were parked cars along there, inside which the virgins of Miraflores became reckless and surrendered. Couples could also be seen leaning against the guardrail near the precipice. Alfredo walked awhile with the black girl and finally sat down on the wall.

"Don't you want to look at the ocean?" he asked. "If we jump over to the other side, we'll be only a step away from the edge."

"What will people say!" the girl protested.

"You're more bourgeois than I am! . . . Come on! Follow me! Everyone comes for a look at the ocean."

After helping her over the railing, they walked a bit on level ground until they reached the edge of the precipice. The sound of the ocean rose untiringly, terrifyingly. Down below the white foam of the waves was breaking against the rocky beach. The wind made the pair teeter.

"What if we commit suicide?" asked Alfredo. "It would be the best way to avenge ourselves of all this garbage."

"You jump first and I'll follow you," the black girl laughed.

"You're beginning to understand me," Alfredo said, and grabbing the girl by the shoulders, he quickly kissed her on the lips.

Then they started back. Alfredo felt an incomprehensible restlessness growing inside him. They were jumping over the guardrail when a powerful beam of light blinded them. The sound of car doors violently opening and closing could be heard and soon two policemen were in front of them.

"What were you doing down below? Let's see some identification."

Alfredo felt around in his pockets and came up with his I.D. card.

"You've been fooling around with her on the cliff, haven't you?"

"We went to look at the ocean."

"They're pulling your leg," the other policeman intervened. "Let's take them in. At this hour a man doesn't come to look at the ocean with a person of modest color."

Alfredo felt like laughing again. "Let's see," he said walking up to the policeman. "What do you mean by people of modest color? Are you saying that this young lady can't be my girlfriend?"

"She can't be."

"Why not?"

"Because she's colored."

Alfredo laughed again. "Now I understand why you're a policeman!"

Some other couples were walking along the levee. They were white. The officers didn't pay any attention to them.

"And those people, why don't you ask them for some identification?"

"We're not here to argue. Get in the patrol car!"

Situations like these were resolved in only one way: with money. Alfredo, however, didn't have a penny in his pocket. "I'd be more than happy to get in," he said. "But let the young lady go."

This time the policeman didn't respond but rather grabbed them both by the arms and forced them inside the car. "To the station!" they ordered the driver.

Alfredo lit a cigarette. His sense of unrest grew worse. The ocean air had stimulated his mental awareness. The situation seemed unacceptable to him and he was getting ready to protest when he felt the black girl's hand reach for his. He squeezed it. "Nothing's going to happen," he told her, trying to reassure her.

It was Saturday and the police chief must have gone out carousing because the only one there was the officer of day duty, playing chess with a friend. Getting up, he walked a circle around Alfredo and the black girl, looking them over from head to toe.

"Aren't you a hooker?" he asked, blowing a puff of smoke in the girl's face. "Where do you work?"

"The young lady is my friend," Alfredo broke in. "She works at José Gálvez' home. I can vouch for her."

"And who can vouch for you?"

"You can make a phone call and ask about me."

"Fooling around at the levee is prohibited," the officer continued. "Do you know that it is an offense to go against established social norms? There's a book called Penal Code and it talks about that."

"I don't know if you'd call walking with a friend an offense."

"In the dark, yes, and more so with a colored girl."

"They were hugging, lieutenant," a policeman joined in.

"Don't you see? This could cost you twenty-four hours in jail and a photo of her could come out in *Ultima Hora*."

"This is all ludicrous!" Alfredo exclaimed, impatiently. "Why don't you let us go? Besides, I tell you this young woman is my girlfriend."

"Your girlfriend!" The officer broke out laughing, his jaw flapping up and down while the policemen imitated him out of habit. Suddenly he stopped laughing and looked pensive.

"You don't think I'm stupid," he said as he came up to Alfredo. "I may wear a uniform, but even I have a little bit of culture. Why don't we try something? Since this young woman is your girlfriend, go ahead and take her for a stroll. But not on the levee because they could attack you there. How about if we go to Salazar Park? We'll escort you in the patrol car."

Alfredo hesitated a moment. "That's fine with me," he answered.

"Go ahead, then!" the lieutenant laughed. "Take them to Salazar Park!"

Back in the patrol car, Alfredo kept quiet. He was thinking about the park's unmerciful lighting, a kind of showcase for the surrounding residential beauty. The black girl reached for his hand, but this time Alfredo squeezed it without conviction.

"I'm embarrassed," she whispered in his ear.

"Nonsense!" he answered.

"For you, I'm embarrassed for you!"

Alfredo tried to show her a little affection but the park lights came into view.

"Just let us out here," he told the policemen. "We promise to take a stroll through the park."

The patrol car stopped about a hundred yards away.

"We'll watch awhile," they said.

Alfredo and the black girl got out. Skirting the embankment, they began to approach the park. The black girl had timidly taken his arm as she walked beside him, without looking up, as if she too were being subjected to an incomprehensible humiliation. Alfredo, on the other hand, saying nothing, never took his eyes off that compact multitude walking around the gardens and from which was emanating an happy, growing murmur. He saw first the faces of the pretty girls of Miraflores, the elegant sweaters of the good-looking guys, their aunts' cars, buses unloading groups of young people, all part of that carefree, obstreperous, triumphant, irresponsible, despotic, and judgmental world. All of his courage suddenly vanished as if he had ventured out onto an angry sea.

"Look," he said. "I'm out of cigarettes. I'm going to the corner but I'll be back. Wait for me a minute."

Before the black girl could respond, he had left the sidewalk, crossed between two cars and quickly fled, hunched over, as if threatened with a shower of stones from behind. About a hundred feet away he suddenly stopped and looked back. From there he saw the black girl who, without waiting for him, was moving away with her head down and her hand caressing the rough, low wall surrounding the park.

PARIS, 1961

The Substitute Teacher

❧❧❧❧❧❧❧❧❧❧❧❧

*L*ate one afternoon, Matías and his wife sat sipping clear tea and complaining about all the poverty of the middle class—always having to go around in a clean shirt, the cost of bus fare, the red tape—in short, those things struggling couples normally talk about at the end of the day, when they heard a loud knocking at the door. As soon as they opened it, Doctor Valencia burst through, cane in hand and choking because of his starched collar.

"My dear Matías! I've got some great news for you! From now on you will be a teacher! Wait! Don't say no. Since I'm going to have to be out of the country for a few months, I've decided to give you my history classes at the academy. It's no big deal, of course, and the salary isn't that great, but it would be the perfect chance for you to get some teaching experience. In time you could probably get more teaching hours in other schools and, who knows, you could go on to teach at the university level. That's up to you. I've always had a lot of confidence in you. I don't think it's fair that a man of your ability, a distinguished man, an educated person like yourself, should have to earn a living as a bill collector. No sir, that's not right and I'm the first to say so. You belong in the teaching profession. Don't think twice about it. I'm going to call the principal right away and tell him I've found a replacement. I'm in a big hurry. A taxi is waiting for me. Give me a hug, Matías, and tell me I'm your friend!"

Before Matías could utter a word, Doctor Valencia had called the academy, talked with the director, embraced him for the fourth time, and had blown out the door like the wind without ever having taken off his hat.

For several minutes Matías stood quietly, stroking his handsome bald head that had always inspired laughter in children and struck terror in the hearts of housewives. With a quick gesture he silenced his wife before she could interject a comment; then he quietly went to the china closet and helped himself to some good port that he usually reserved for guests. After inspecting it against the lamplight, he savored it slowly.

"This really doesn't surprise me," he said finally. "A man of my qualifications can't hide his light under a bushel forever."

After supper he closed himself up in the dining room, had a pot of coffee brought in, began dusting off his old schoolbooks, and ordered his wife not to let anybody disturb him, not even his two buddies from work, Baltázar and Luciano, with whom he would frequently get together in the evenings to play cards and crack impudent jokes about their supervisors at work.

By ten o'clock the next morning, Matías had prepared the first lesson well and left the apartment after impatiently dodging his solicitous wife, who followed him down the hall, picking lint off his formal suit.

"Don't forget to put the card on the door," Matías reminded her as he left. "Put it where it can be seen: 'Matías Palomino, Professor of History.'"

On the way he passed the time by mentally reviewing the lesson. The night before he couldn't help but shiver with delight when, while brushing up on Louis XVI, he came across the epithet *Hydra*. It was a nineteenth-century term that had fallen into disuse, but Matías, by his bearing and reading, still belonged to the nineteenth century, and his intellilgence— whenever the subject came up—had similarly fallen into disuse. For the past twelve years, ever since he had twice failed his examinations for the bachelor's degree, he hadn't opened a single textbook, nor had he felt the least bit motivated to revive his suppressed quest for knowledge. He always attributed his failure in academics to the general hostility of the examining committee, and to the unfortunate attack of amnesia he suffered whenever called upon to demonstrate his knowledge. Since becoming a lawyer was out of the question, he had chosen the prose and necktie of a court clerk; that way, at least by appearance, if not by knowledge, he stayed within the boundaries of the profession.

When Matías arrived in front of the school, he stopped abruptly and noticed in himself a feeling of bewilderment. The huge clock on the building indicated he was ten minutes early. Thinking it would be somewhat unfashionable to be too punctual, he decided to walk to the corner. As he passed in front of the school gate he noticed a rather stern-looking porter who was apparently guarding the entrance, his hands clasped behind his back.

At the corner of the park, Matías paused, took out his handkerchief and mopped his forehead. It was a little warm outside. The shadows of a pine and a palm tree converged in a way that reminded him of a poem whose author he tried in vain to remember. He was getting ready to head back—the clock at City Hall had just struck eleven o'clock—when he saw a pale man staring at him from behind the display window of a record shop. Startled, he suddenly realized that it was nothing more than his own reflection. Observing himself carefully, he gave a wink, as if to smooth away the tired, gloomy lines that a long night of cramming and coffee had etched on his face. But his expression, far from disappearing, began to reveal even more. Matías could see that his bald pate was sadly shining between the tufts at his temples, and that his mustache was drooping over his lips in a gesture of total defeat.

Unnerved by what he saw, he impulsively stepped back from the glass. The morning heat forced him to loosen his satin necktie. Finding himself once again at the school entrance, he was seized by a tremendous sensation of uncertainty, seemingly without any warning or provocation. Suddenly he couldn't be sure if the Hydra was a marine animal, a mythological monster, or simply one of Doctor Valencia's inventions, one of those imaginary figures the professor would sometimes use to intimidate members of parliament who opposed him. Confused, he opened his briefcase and began to review his notes. That was when he noticed the doorman was eyeing him. That kind of gaze, coming from a man in uniform, sparked such a series of dreadful associations in his small, taxpayer's psyche that he couldn't stop himself, and he kept walking to the opposite street corner.

He stood there a moment almost gasping for breath. The doubts about the Hydra no longer interested him. They had only dredged up other, more pressing doubts. Everything became a blur in his head. He was mistaking Colbert for an English minister, placing Marat's hunchback on the shoulders of Robespierre, and by some trick of the imagination, Chenier's fine Alexandrian verse started flowing from the lips of the powerful Samson. Terrified by this disorderly rush of ideas, his eyes madly searched for a bar. He was dying of thirst.

For the next fifteen minutes he wandered aimlessly through nearby winding streets in a residential area where beauty salons abounded. After circling countless times, he stumbled on the record store and again saw his image appear in the glass. This time Matías examined it more carefully: two black rings had formed around his eyes and that circle could only be the circle of terror.

Flustered, he turned around and stood viewing the park. His fluttering heart made his head bob like a caged bird. Although the hands on the clock kept turning forward, Matías stood rigid, obsessed with insignificant things, like counting the number of branches on a tree, and trying to decipher an advertisement on a store sign partially hidden by foliage.

The loud bong of the church bell brought him to his senses, and he realized he still had time. Pulling himself together by exchanging stubbornness for conviction, yet upset by lost time, he took off toward the school. Movement stimulated his courage. As the school entrance came into view, he took on the serious air of an important businessman. He was about to go in when, looking up, he saw next to the doorman a conclave of gray-haired, restless old men in robes who were eyeing him impatiently. This unexpected group—a reminder of the school examiners from his childhood who examined him—was enough to unleash a flood of defense mechanisms and, turning around, he fled toward the street.

Barely twenty steps out he realized that someone was following him. It was the doorman. "Excuse me," he said. "Aren't you Mr. Palomino, the new history professor? The brothers are waiting for you."

Matías whirled around, red with anger. "I'm a bill collector!" he lashed out, as if he'd been the victim of some bad joke.

The doorman apologized and left. Matías kept walking until he reached the avenue, then he turned toward the park and walked aimlessly among the shoppers; he tripped over a curb, nearly knocked down a blind man, and finally, befuddled and flushed, he slumped down on a bench, feeling as if his brain were made of cheese.

The sounds of children at play that afternoon roused him from his lethargy. Still confused and feeling as though he'd been the object of a humiliating practical joke, he got to his feet and started for home. Unconsciously he chose a route that meandered here and there. He was distracted. Reality slipped away from him through the cracks in his imagination. He imagined how some day, by some unforeseen stroke of luck, he would strike it rich. Not until he made it back to the apartment and saw his wife waiting for him at the door, an apron tied around her waist, was he aware of his enormous sense of frustration. Nevertheless, he regained his composure, attempted a smile, and hurried to greet his wife, who by then was running down the hallway with open arms.

"How did it go? Did you teach your class? What did your students say?"

"Great! It was really terrific!" he babbled. "They loved me!" But when he felt his wife's arms around his neck and saw in her eyes—for the first time—a flicker of immense pride, he dropped his head and began sorrowfully to sob.

BELGIUM, 1957

The Insignia

I still remember that afternoon when I was walking along the levee and discovered a shiny object in a small trash pile. With a curiosity easily explained by my collector's temperament, I bent over to pick it up, and rubbed it against my coat sleeve. I saw that it was a tiny, silver pin engraved with symbols that seemed meaningless to me at the time. I put it in my pocket, and without giving it another thought, I went home. It's hard to say how long it stayed there in my coat pocket, since I seldom wore that suit. I only know that one day I sent it to the cleaners and, when I went to pick it up, much to my surprise the clerk also handed me a little box, and said: "This must be yours. I found it in your pocket."

It was the pin, of course. Its sudden reappearance impressed me so much that I decided to wear it.

That's really when I started to become involved in a series of bizarre events. The first took place in an old bookstore. I was examining a collection of old books when the owner, who had been observing me from the darkest corner of the store, came up, and in a low, conspiratorial tone, amid winks and grimaces, said, "We have some of Feifer's books here." I gave him an inquisitive look because I hadn't asked about that author and, although I know my knowledge of literature isn't that broad, I hadn't even heard of him. Then the man suddenly added: "Feifer was in Pilsen." Seeing that I was still stunned, he finished saying in a secretive, hushed voice, "You must know that they killed him. Yes, he was bludgeoned to death with a cane in Prague." Having said this, he withdrew into the same corner from which he had emerged and kept perfectly quiet. I absentmindedly continued looking through some volumes, but my thoughts kept going back to the bookseller's mysterious words. After buying a little book on mechanics, I left the store, a bit unnerved.

For a long time I tried to figure out the meaning of that incident, but finally I gave up and ended up forgetting all about it. Not long after that something else happened that really shook me up. I was walking across a plaza in one of the suburbs when a small man with a jaundiced, angular face accidentally bumped into me and, before I could react, he slipped a card in my hand, then disappeared without a word. The card, written on smooth, white cardboard, contained only an address and a message that read: SECOND SESSION: TUESDAY 4TH. As you may have guessed, on Tuesday the fourth I showed up at the address noted on the card. I saw several unusual people wandering around outside the meeting place who, oddly enough, were wearing pins just like mine. I joined the group and noticed that they all greeted me like old friends. Almost immediately we went inside the building and sat down in a big room. A man with a serious look on his face came out from behind a curtain, greeted us, and began delivering a lengthy speech from a platform. I don't know exactly what he was lecturing about; I don't even know if it could really be described as a lecture. He began stringing together his childhood memories interspersed with several reflective philosophical comments, which appeared to give a sense of unity to his talk: he applied the same interpretive method when he digressed about the cultivation of sugar beets as when he expounded on government organization. I remember he ended his talk by drawing red lines on a blackboard with a piece of chalk he pulled from his pocket.

As soon as he finished, everyone got up and began to leave while enthusiastically commenting on the great success of the speech. I felt obliged to add my praises to theirs. But as I was about to go out the door, the speaker excitedly called out to me and, turning around, I saw him signal me to come forward.

"You're new, right?" he asked me with a hint of skepticism.

"Yes," I replied with some hesitation. The truth is, I was surprised that he could single me out from among so many people. "I've never been here before."

"Who introduced you?"

Fortunately I remembered the bookstore incident. "I was in the bookstore on Amargura Street when he . . ."

"Who? Martín?"

"Yes, Martín."

"Ah, he is a great associate of ours!"

"I'm one of his oldest customers."

"What did you talk about?"

"Well, about Feifer."

"What did he tell you?"

"That he had been in Pilsen. Frankly . . . I didn't know about it."

"You didn't know?"

"No," I answered, trying to keep my composure.

"And you didn't know that they beat him to death at the Prague station?"

"He told me that, too."

"Ah, it was a terrifying thing for us!"

"It certainly was," I assured him. "It was an irreparable loss."

Somehow we kept up a vague, casual dialogue complete with deep secrets and shallow allusions, like the dialogue between two strangers who by chance find themselves sitting together on a bus. I recall that while I was struggling to describe for him my tonsillectomy, he was using grand gestures to illustrate the beauty of the Nordic countries. Finally, before I left, he gave me an assignment that I'll never forget.

"Next week bring me a list of all the telephone numbers beginning with 38," he said.

I promised to carry out his order. Before the week was over I handed him the list.

"Amazing!" he exclaimed, "You work at a speed we could all learn from."

From that day on I've had similar tasks of the strangest sort. For example, one time I had to locate a dozen parrots which I never saw again. Later I was sent to a provincial city to make a sketch of a municipal building. I've also had to throw banana peels at the door of a few, carefully selected homes, to write an article on the heavenly bodies—which I never saw published—and to train a monkey in parliamentary procedure. I've even had to carry out a number of secret missions like delivering letters I never read, or spying on exotic women in the habit of disappearing without a trace.

Gradually I began making a name for myself. At the end of one year I was promoted during a thrilling ceremony. "You've moved up a step," my superior informed me, embracing me warmly. I then delivered a short speech in which I made vague references to our common goal. Nevertheless, my comments were heartily received.

At home, however, everything was in turmoil. My family couldn't understand my sudden absences and my mysterious deeds. I would avoid answering their many questions because, quite frankly, it was impossible to find an acceptable response. Several relatives even encouraged me to see a psychiatrist, since my behavior wasn't exactly that of a reasonable man. One time especially comes to mind. It was the day they caught me making twelve dozen false mustaches, another assignment I'd been given by my boss.

All this domestic flack didn't stop me from throwing myself into the work of our society, with a passion that even I found mystifying. Soon I became reporter, treasurer, conference coordinator, and administrative advisor. As I got to be more and more indispensible to the organization's network, I became extremely distressed, not sure if I was part of a religious sect or a member of a cloth manufacturers' union.

After three years they sent me abroad. The trip was an intriguing adventure. I didn't have a cent, but I was offered the staterooms aboard ships, someone welcomed me at every port and attended to all my needs, and hotels gave me free lodging. I made contacts with other associates, learned foreign languages, gave lectures, conducted initiations, and watched as the silver insignia circulated all over the continent. When I came back home after this year of intense personal experience, I was as perplexed as that day I walked into Martín's bookstore.

Ten years have gone by since then. Through hard work I've become president. During special ceremonies I make an appearance wearing a robe trimmed in purple. Members say Your Excellency when addressing me. I have an income of five thousand dollars, several summer homes, servants in crisp uniforms who both respect and fear me, and even a mistress. Despite all this, today, like the first day and always, I live in a state of total ignorance. If someone should ask me what our organization stands for, I wouldn't know what to say. All I can do is faithfully continue to draw red lines on a blackboard, trusting that eventually someone will come up with an explanation that always has its origin, of course, in life's capricious, cabalistic nature.

LIMA, 1952

The Banquet

*D*on Fernando Pasamano had begun planning in great detail this major social event two months ahead of time. For starters, his home would have to be completely renovated. Since it was a big, outdated structure, several partitions had to be torn down, windows enlarged, wooden floors replaced, and all the walls repainted. These changes made others necessary, of course—like when someone buys himself a new pair of shoes and decides that, if he's to show them off properly, he'll also need new socks, shirt, suit, and finally new underwear—Don Fernando felt compelled to replace all the furniture, from the living room consoles to a bench for the pantry. Then came new rugs, lamps, draperies, and paintings to cover the walls that somehow seemed larger and bleaker after the paint job. Finally, he would have to add a garden, since an outdoor concert was listed on the program. In just fifteen days a team of Japanese gardeners transformed what used to be a wild orchard into a fabulous rococo garden with sculptured cypress trees, intricate little pathways, a pond stocked with goldfish, a grotto for the goddesses, and a quaint wooden bridge spanning an imaginary brook.

The most troublesome detail, however, was deciding on a menu. Like the majority of Peruvians born and raised in the nation's interior, Don Fernando and his wife had only attended large, rural feasts where *chicha*,[1] the traditional drink, was mixed with whiskey and where hands, instead of forks, were used to finish off portions of the cavies that were always devoured at these events. That's why Don Fernando was confused about what to serve at the banquet he would be giving in the president's honor. All his relatives who gathered to discuss this matter only added to the confusion. Finally, Don Fernando decided to poll Lima's finest hotels and restaurants. That's how he found out about presidential cuisine and, of course, the fine wines that he would need to have flown in from the southern vineyards.

When all these details had been worked out, Don Fernando nervously had to confess that he had invested his entire fortune in this banquet which would involve one hundred and fifty guests, forty waiters, two orchestras, a ballet troupe, and a movie cameraman. But in the long run,

1. *Chicha* is an alcoholic drink made from maize.

the expense would seem insignificant compared to the enormous benefits he would receive by hosting the elaborate affair.

"With an ambassadorship in Europe and railroad service to my property in the sierra we will rebuild our fortune in the wink of an eye," he would tell his wife. "That's all I ask. I'm a modest man."

"We don't even know if the president will come," his wife replied.

The fact is, Don Fernando had not yet invited him. He felt fairly certain for now that he would accept his invitation, reassuring himself with the knowledge that he, after all, was kin to the president, one of those rather vague kinships so common in mountainous regions, and yet, somewhat difficult to prove for fear of discovering in the process some evidence of illegitimacy. Nevertheless, just to be sure, he found the opportunity—during his first visit to the presidential palace—to take the president aside and humbly tell him about the invitation.

"I'd be delighted," the president responded. "It's a wonderful idea. I have a busy schedule right now, but I'll confirm my acceptance in writing a little later."

Don Fernando began waiting impatiently for the letter of confirmation. Meanwhile, he ordered some last-minute touches that gave his mansion an unnatural, garish look, like a palace decorated for a masquerade ball. His last idea was to commission a portrait of the president—painted by an artist from a photograph—which he made sure was hung in a prominent place in the house.

The letter arrived at the end of four weeks and transformed Don Fernando's growing doubts into overwhelming joy. It was a day to celebrate, and just the beginning! Before going to bed, he and his wife stepped out on the balcony to view the luminous garden and savor the pastoral vision that would be forever etched in their memory. The countryside, however, almost seemed to exceed the bounds of ordinary sensibility. Everywhere Don Fernando looked he saw himself in a cutaway coat, smoking cigars against a background that looked a lot like travel posters, where monuments of Europe's four most important cities all begin to look the same. In a distant corner of this vision, he could see a train returning from the tropics with a cargo of gold. He saw himself surrounded by sensuality itself in the form of an elusive, transparent feminine figure with long, sexy legs, a regal hat, and Tahitian eyes—not at all like his wife.

On the day of the banquet the first to arrive were the presidential bodyguards. From five o'clock that afternoon they posted themselves outside, making every effort to hide their identity. This was impossible, of course, because their hats and exaggerated look of indifference gave them away, especially the disgusting display of shiftiness often acquired by detectives, spies, and others who perform undercover operations.

Later, cars started to arrive from which emerged heads of state, members of parliament, diplomats, businessmen, and intellectuals. An attendant received them at the gate, an usher announced them, a valet took their wraps, and Don Fernando, in the middle of the hall, shook their hands while murmuring polite words of welcome appropriate for such an occasion.

When all the local bourgeoisie and people from the tenement houses had crowded in front of the mansion and were getting caught up in the luster of this unexpected event, the president arrived. Escorted by his military aides, he walked immediately into the house, causing Don Fernando, who was suddenly moved by the intimacy of that moment, to lose control and forget protocol; he threw his arms around the chief executive with such fervor that he crushed one of the epaulets on his uniform.

The guests, who were scattered throughout the spacious rooms, hallways, terraces, and gardens, discretely consumed—between exchanges of wit and humor—all forty cases of whiskey. Later they gravitated toward the tables and chairs that had been reserved for them and made themselves comfortable. The largest table, decorated with orchids, was occupied by the president and other important figures who began to eat and boisterously talk while, in one corner of the hall, the orchestra was making a futile attempt to perform a Viennese waltz.

Halfway through the meal, after white wine from the Rhine region had been raised in a toast and the Mediterranean red wine began to fill the glasses, a round of eloquent speeches began. The oratory broke off, however, when the pheasant was served and didn't start up again until after the champagne was poured; the final eulogies trickled on through the after-dinner coffee and finally evaporated altogether, much like the cognac.

Through all this Don Fernando couldn't help anxiously noting that the banquet was in full swing, charting its own course, and that he had not yet had a chance to bend the president's ear. Although he had again botched the rules of protocol by seating himself to the left of the honored guest during dinner, he never found the right moment to bring up his plans. What's more, after dinner, people began to get up and form drowsy, listless little groups among which he, as host, felt obligated to circulate and enliven with liqueurs, cigars, mindless chatter, and a friendly pat on the back.

Finally, around midnight, when one of the cabinet members, thoroughly plastered, left in a great deal of commotion, Don Fernando managed to steer the president toward the parlor. There, seated on one of the sofas that in the Versailles court someone probably used to propose to a princess or break an alliance, Don Fernando made his modest requests known.

"No problem at all," responded the president. "In fact, right this minute there's a vacancy in the Rome Embassy. When I meet with my cabinet tomorrow I'll recommend you for the post. Better yet, I'll appoint you. And about the railroad, I can tell you that a congressional commission has been discussing that project for months. Day after tomorrow I'll call a meeting of its members, and you come too so you can help them work out something to your liking."

An hour later the president left after repeating the promises he had made earlier. His cabinet members, the congress, and so on, followed behind him in the customary order.

At two o'clock in the morning there were a few audacious ciphers still hanging around the bar hoping that another bottle of champagne would be uncorked, or that they would have a chance to pilfer a silver ashtray when no one was looking. It was three o'clock when Don Fernando and his wife finally had the house to themselves. They stayed up until dawn sharing impressions and making ambitious plans for the future amid the remaining bits and pieces of their fabulous feast. At last they fell asleep, knowing that never before had someone from Lima thrown a more lavish bash nor so shrewdly risked everything he owned in order to pull it off.

At noon the following day Don Fernando was awakened by his wife's scream. As he opened his eyes he saw her rush into the bedroom with a newspaper spread between her hands. Snatching it from her, he read the headlines, and without uttering a word, he fell back onto the bed in a dead faint. Just before daybreak, a government official, taking advantage of the reception, had led a coup d'etat, forcing the president to resign.

LIMA, 1958

Alienation
(An Instructive Story with a Footnote)

*D*espite the fact that he was a mulatto named López, he longed to resemble less and less a defensive back on the Alianza Lima Soccer Team and increasingly to take on the look of a blond from Philadelphia. Life had taught him that if he wanted to prosper in a colonial city it was better to skip the intermediate stages and transform himself into a gringo from the United States rather than into just a fair-skinned nobody from Lima. During the years that I knew him, he devoted all of his attention to eliminating every trace of the López and zambo[1] within him and Americanizing himself before the bottom fell out and he would turn into, say, a bank guard or a taxi driver. He had to begin by killing the Peruvian in himself and extracting something from every gringo he met. From all this plundering a new person would emerge, a fragmented being who was neither mulatto nor gringo, but rather the result of an unnatural commingling, something that the force of destiny would eventually change, unfortunately for him, from a rosy dream into a hellish nightmare.

But let's not get ahead of ourselves. We should establish the fact that his name was Roberto, that years later he was known as Bobby, but that the most recent official documents refer to him as Bob. At each stage in his frantic ascent toward nothingness his name would lose one syllable.

Everything began the afternoon when a group of us fair-haired kids were playing ball on Bolognesi Plaza. We were out of school on vacation and some of us who lived in nearby chalets, both girls and boys, would meet at the plaza during those endless summer afternoons. Roberto used to go there too, even though he attended a public school and lived on one of the last backstreets left in the district rather than in a chalet. He would go there to watch the girls play and to be greeted by some fair-faced kid who had seen him growing up on those streets and knew he was the laundry woman's son.

In reality, he would go there like the rest of us, to see Queca. We were all infatuated with Queca, who, during the past couple of years, had the distinction of being chosen class queen, an honor bestowed upon her during festivities at the end of the school year. Queca didn't study with the German sisters of Saint Ursula, nor with the North Americans of Villa

---

1. Ribeyro uses the term *zambo* to refer to a person who is a blend of Indian and Negro.

María, but rather with the Spanish nuns of Reparation. That was no big deal, nor the fact that her father was a blue-collar worker who drove a bus, nor that her house had only one story garnished with geraniums instead of roses. What was important then were her rosy skin, her green eyes, her long, brown hair, the way she ran, laughed, jumped, and her incomparable legs, always bare and golden and which, in time, would become legendary.

Roberto used to come only to watch her play; none of the boys who came from the other Miraflores neighborhoods, or even those who later came from San Isidro and Barranco, for that matter, could attract her attention. One time Peluca Rodríguez flung himself from the highest branch of a pine tree; Lucas de Tramontana drove up on a shiny motorcycle that had eight headlights; Fats Gómez broke the nose of the ice cream vendor who had the gall to whistle at us; and Armando Wolff donned several fine, new flannel suits with a bow tie. But not one of them caught Queca's eye. Queca favored no one; she preferred to talk with everybody, to run, skip, laugh, and play volleyball, leaving behind at nightfall a gang of teenage boys overwhelmed by intense sexual frustration that only a charitable hand underneath white sheets was able to console.

It was a fatal ball that someone tossed that afternoon, that Queca was unable to catch, and that rolled toward the bench where Roberto sat alone and observant. He had always waited for this moment. With a jump he landed on the grass, crawled between the flower beds, leaped over the hedge covered with passionflowers, stepped into a drainage ditch, and rescued the ball, which was just about to roll under the wheels of a car. But as he returned with it, Queca, who was now facing him with outstretched hands, seemed to be adjusting her focus, observing something that only now she was really seeing for the first time: a short, dark, thick-lipped being with kinky hair, something very ordinary that she probably saw daily, just as one sees park benches or pine trees. Abruptly, she turned away, terrified.

Roberto never forgot Queca's words as she fled: "I don't play with zambos." These five words decided his destiny.

Every human being who suffers becomes an observer, so Roberto continued going to the plaza for several years, but his look had lost all innocence. It was no longer a simple reflection of the world, but rather an organ of vigilance—penetrating, selecting, and examining.

Queca was growing up; her run was more moderate now, her skirts longer, her leaps weren't quite so bold, and her conduct around the gang had become more distant and selective. We were all aware of these changes, but Roberto observed something more: that Queca tended to turn away from her more swarthy admirers until, through successive comparisons, she focused her attention only on Chalo Sander, the one boy in the group with the fairest hair, the lightest skin, and the only one who studied in a school run by North American priests. By the time her legs were the most triumphant and well-turned, she was speaking exclusively to him. The first time she strolled to the levee holding hands with him we understood that she wasn't part of our turf anymore; there was nothing we could do but play the role of the chorus in a Greek tragedy, always present and visible, but irrecoverably separated from the gods.

Rejected and forlorn, we would gather on the street corner after one of our games, where we would smoke our first cigarettes, arrogantly fondle the newly discovered down of our mustaches, and comment on the hopeless state of things. Sometimes we would go into a bar owned by a Chinese named Manuel and have a beer. Roberto followed us around like a shadow, always scrutinizing us from the doorway, never missing a word of our conversation. Sometimes we would say, "Hi, zambo, have a drink with us," and he always said, "No thanks, another time," and although he smiled and kept his distance, we knew that he shared in his own way our sense of loss.

And it was Chalo Sander, of course, who took Queca to the graduation party when we finished high school. We decided to meet in our favorite bar early that evening. We drank more than usual, plotted bizarre schemes, and spoke of kidnapping, of planning some kind of group attack. But it was all just talk. By eight o'clock we were in front of the modest little house with geraniums, resigned to being witnesses of our own privation. Chalo arrived in his father's car, sporting an elegant white tuxedo; a few minutes later he left the house accompanied by Queca, who, with her long evening gown and upswept hairdo, hardly resembled our once playful classmate. Queca, smiling and clutching a satin evening purse, didn't even see us. An elusive vision, the last, because never again would things be the same. All of our hopes died instantly, at that very moment that would never let us forget the indelible image that brought to a close a part of our youth.

Almost no one hung around the plaza anymore, some because they were getting ready to enroll at the university, others because they were moving to other neighborhoods in search of an impossible replica of Queca. Only Roberto, who was now a delivery boy for a bakery, returned to the plaza at nightfall, where other young boys and girls now became the new gang and played our games so naturally that it seemed as if they had invented them. Sitting on his solitary bench, Roberto appeared to pay little attention to the goings on around him, but in reality his eyes were always fixed upon Queca's house. That way he was able to confirm before anyone else that Chalo had been only one episode in Queca's life, a kind of rehearsal preparing her for the arrival of the original, of which Chalo had been a mere copy: Billy Mulligan, the son of a United States consulate official.

Billy was freckled, redheaded, wore flowered shirts, had enormous feet, a boisterous laugh, and the sun, instead of toasting him, made him peel; but he always came to see Queca in his own car and not in his father's car. Nobody knew where Queca first met him nor how he came to be there, but she began to see him often, until she saw only him—his tennis rackets, his sunglasses, his camera—while the outline of Chalo gradually grew more and more opaque, smaller, and more distant until it finally disappeared altogether. Moving from the group to the type, the type to the individual, Queca had shown her hand. Only Mulligan would take her to the altar and, when they were lawfully married, he would have every right to caress those thighs we had dreamed about in vain for so long.

Deception generally is something that no one can tolerate; it's either soon forgotten, its causes evaded, or it becomes the object of ridicule and even a theme in literature. It turned out that Fats Gómez went off to study in London, Peluca Rodríguez wrote a really ballsy sonnet, Armando Wolff came to the conclusion that Queca was nothing but a social climber, and Lucas de Tramontana deceitfully boasted that he had laid her several times out on the levee. Roberto was the only one who learned a true, valuable lesson from all this; it had to be Mulligan or no one. What good was it to be blond if there were so many light-skinned braggarts who were desperate, lazy, and failures? There had to be a superior state, inhabited by those who could plan their lives with confidence in this gray city and who could effortlessly reap all the best fruits the land had to offer. The problem was how to become another Mulligan, since he was a zambo. But suffering, when it doesn't kill, sharpens ingenuity; so Roberto subjected himself to a long, thorough analysis and outlined a plan of action.

First of all he had to dezambofy himself. His hair wasn't a major problem; he dyed it with peroxide and had it straightened. As for his skin, he tried mixed starch, rice powder, and talcum from the drugstore until he found the ideal combination; but a dyed and powdered zambo is still a zambo. He needed to know how the North American gringos dressed, talked, moved, and thought; in short, exactly who they were.

Back then we saw Roberto marauding about during his free time in various locales that seemingly had nothing in common, except for one thing: they were usually frequented by gringos. Some saw him standing in front of the Country Club, others at the Santa María school gates; and Lucas de Tramontana swore that he caught a glimpse of him behind a fence at the golf course, and someone else spotted him at the airport trying to carry some tourist's luggage; and then there were several who found him roaming about the halls of the U.S. Embassy.

This phase of his plan was for him absolutely perfect. For the moment, he was able to see that the gringos were set apart from others by the special way they dressed, which he described as sporty, comfortable, and unconventional. Hence, Roberto was one of the first to discover the advantages of blue jeans, the virile cowboy look of the wide leather belt fastened by an enormous buckle, the soft comfort of white canvas shoes with rubber soles, the collegiate charm of a canvas cap with a visor, the coolness of a flowered or striped short-sleeved shirt, the variety of nylon jackets zipped up in front, or the sporty shirts displaying provocative, carefree slogans along with the logo of an American university.

None of these articles of clothing were sold in any department store but had to be brought from the United States, impossible for him to do. But, checking around, he discovered garage sales. Prior to returning to the United States, gringo families would announce in the newspaper their intention to sell everything they had. Roberto showed up on their doorstep before anyone else, acquiring in this way a wardrobe in which he invested himself and his life's savings.

With hair that was now straightened and bleached, a pair of blue jeans and a loud shirt, Roberto was on the brink of becoming Bobby.

All of this created problems. His mother said that no one would speak to him on the street, thinking he was pretentious. What was even worse, they would make jokes or whistle at him as if he were a queer. He never contributed a cent for food, he would stand for hours in front of the mirror, and he spent all his money on old clothing. His father, according to Roberto's black mother, may have been a worthless scoundrel who, like the magical Fu Man Chu, vanished only a year after they met, but at least he was never embarrassed to be seen with her, nor was he ashamed of being a pilot's mate on a boat.

In our group the first one to notice the change in Roberto was Peluca Rodríguez, who had ordered a pair of blue jeans through a Braniff purser. When the jeans came, he put them on and headed for the plaza to show them off, only to run into Roberto, who was wearing a pair identical to his. For days he did nothing but curse the zambo, saying he had ruined his act, that he had probably been spying on him to copy him. He even noticed that he bought Lucky Strike cigarettes and that he combed his hair with a lock falling over his forehead.

But the worst thing concerned his job. Cahuide Morales, the owner of the bakery, was a gruff, big-bellied, provincial mestizo who loved cracklings and native waltzes; and one who had broken his back for the last twenty years to make the business go. Nothing annoyed him more than for someone to pretend to be what he wasn't. Whether one was a mixed-breed or white didn't matter: what was important was *mosca, agua, molido*: He knew a thousand different words for money. When he saw that his employee had bleached his hair, he endured another wrinkle on his forehead; when he realized that Roberto had actually covered himself with powder, he swallowed a damn word that just about gave him indigestion; but when he came to work dressed like a gringo, the mixture of father, police, bully, and boss broke loose in him and he took Roberto by the scruff of the neck to the back of the store; Morales Brothers' Bakery was a serious business, and one would have to obey the rules; he had overlooked the makeup, but if he didn't come to work in uniform like the other delivery boys, he was going to boot him out the door with a swift kick in the ass.

Roberto was already on a roll and he couldn't go back now; he preferred the kick in the rear.

Those gloomy days were interminable as he looked for another job. His ambition was to go to work in a gringo's home as a butler, gardener, chauffeur, or whatever, but the doors were always shut in his face. His strategy lacked something, and that was a knowledge of English. Since he didn't have funds to enroll in a language academy, he bought himself a dictionary and began copying the words into a notebook. When he reached the letter *C* he threw in the towel; this purely visual knowledge of English wasn't getting him anywhere; but, then, there were always the movies, a school that would not only teach but also entertain.

In the balconies of the premier theaters he spent entire afternoons watching westerns and detective films in the target language. The plots were irrelevant; what mattered was the way the characters spoke. He wrote down all of the words he could understand and then repeated them until they were permanently recorded in his memory. By forcing himself to watch the films over and over again, he learned complete sentences and even entire speeches. In his room in front of the mirror he was suddenly the romantic cowboy making an irresistible declaration of love to the dance-hall girl, or the ruthless gangster uttering a death sentence while riddling his adversary with bullets. Besides, the movies nourished in him certain illusions that filled him with hope, leading him to believe he had discovered in himself a slight resemblance to Alan Ladd, who had appeared in one of the westerns dressed in blue jeans and a red and black plaid jacket. In reality, the only thing he had in common with him was his height and the yellow lock of hair he let dangle over his forehead. Dressed the same as the actor, he saw the film ten times in a row, always standing at the movie entrance after each showing, waiting for people to leave and hoping to overhear them say, but look, how strange, that guy looks like Alan Ladd. No one said it, of course; and the first time we saw him striking that pose, we laughed in his face.

His mother told us one day that finally Roberto had found a job, not in the home of a gringo as he had hoped, but possibly something better: the Miraflores Bowling Club. He waited tables in the bar from five o'clock in the afternoon until midnight. The few times that we went there we saw him excelling diligently. He waited on the natives in an unbiased, frankly impeccable manner, but with the gringos he was ingratiating and servile. As soon as one came in he was at his side, taking his order, and seconds later the customer had received his hot dog and Coca-Cola. He was encouraged to use words in English and, as he was answered in the same language, his vocabulary grew. Soon he possessed a good repertoire of expressions with which he won over the gringos who were delighted to see a native who understood them. Since Roberto was difficult to pronounce, the gringos were the ones who decided to call him Bobby.

And with the name Bobby López he was finally able to enroll in the Peruvian–North American Institute. Those who saw him during that period say that he was the classic bookworm, the kind who never missed a class, or forgot his homework, or hesitated to question the teacher about some obscure grammatical concept. Apart from the white students who for professional reasons were taking courses there, he met others like himself who, although total strangers from different backgrounds and other neighborhoods, nourished the same dreams and led a life similar to his. He especially became a good friend of José María Cabanillas, a tailor's son from Surquillo. Cabanillas shared the same blind admiration for the gringos that he did, and years ago he too had begun to smother the zambo in himself with really enviable results. Besides having the advantage of being taller and lighter-skinned than Bobby, he resembled not Alan Ladd, who after all was a second-rate actor admired by a small group of snobbish girls, but rather the indestructible John Wayne. The two of them made an inseparable pair. They finished out the year with the best grades, and Mr. Brown held them up as examples to the rest of the students, speaking of "their sincere desire to excel."

As buddies they must have had long, pleasant conversations together. They were always going here and there, their rear ends stuffed into faded blue jeans, and always speaking in English to one another. But it's also true that no one could stomach them; they muddled things so badly that neither relatives nor friends could put up with them. That's why they rented a room in a building on Mogollón Avenue, where they lived together. It was there they created a sacred haven that allowed them to mix foreign culture with their own and to feel that in the middle of this dismal city they were living in a California neighborhood. Each one contributed what he could: Bobby, his posters, and José María, who was a music fan, his Frank Sinatra, Dean Martin, and Tommy Dorsey records. What a fine pair of gringos they made, stretched out on the sofa-bed, smoking their Lucky Strikes while listening to "Strangers in the Night" and staring at the bridge over the Hudson River stuck to the wall. With one big try, hop, they would be walking across that bridge.

Even for us it was difficult to travel to the United States. One had to have a scholarship, or relatives already there, or lots of money. For López and Cabanillas, none of these were possible. They saw no other way out but to cut loose like other near-whites, thanks to jobs as airline pursers. Every year when openings were announced, they both applied. They knew more English than anyone else, liked serving others, were self-sacrificing and enthusiastic; but nobody knew them, nobody recommended them, and it was obvious to the interviewers that they were dealing with powdered zambos. They were turned down.

They say that Bobby wept and pulled out his hair and that Cabanillas attempted suicide by jumping from a modest second-floor window. Within their refuge on Mogollón Avenue they spent the darkest days of their lives; the city, which had always sheltered them, had turned into a dirty rag they covered with insults and scorn. But eventually their spirits lifted and new plans surfaced. Since no one wanted anything to do with them here, they would have to get out any way they could. They had no choice but to immigrate disguised as tourists.

For an entire year they worked hard and deprived themselves of everything in order to save enough for their fare and set up a common fund that would allow them to survive abroad. As a result, the two of them were finally able to pack their bags and abandon forever that detested city in which they had suffered so much and to which they never wanted to return as long as they lived.

It's easy to predict the events that followed, and it doesn't take much imagination to complete this parable. In the neighborhood we had direct sources of information: letters from Bobby to his mother, news from travelers abroad, and finally the whole story from a witness.

Soon Bobby and José María spent in one month what they had thought would last them six months. They soon realized that all the Lópezes and Cabanillases in the entire world had congregated in New York—Asians, Arabs, Aztecs, Africans, Iberians, Mayans, Chibchas, Sicilians, Carribeans, Mussulmans, Quechuas, Polynesians, Eskimos, representatives of every origin, language, race, and pigmentation—all of whom had one common goal: the desire to live as a Yankee, for which they had surrendered their souls and altered their appearances. The city tolerated them for several months, complacently, while it absorbed the dollars they had saved. Then, as if through a tube, it led them toward the mechanism of expulsion.

With great difficulty, they got an extension on their visas, while looking for steady jobs that would let them keep up with all the Quecas of the place; and there were many, although the girls just paraded in front of them, paying less attention to them than a cockroach would deserve. They wore out their clothes, Frank Sinatra's music became intolerable, and the mere thought of having to eat another hot dog, which was a luxury in Lima, turned their stomachs. From their cheap hotel they moved first to the Catholic shelter and then to a bench in a public park. Soon they discovered that white substance that fell from the sky, lightened their skin, and made them skate like idiots on the icy sidewalks, a substance which, by its very color, was nature's deceptive racist.

There was only one solution. Thousands of miles away, in a country called Korea, blond North Americans were fighting against some horrible Asians. According to the newspapers, the freedom of Western nations was in jeopardy and statesmen confirmed it on television. But it was so painful to send "the boys" to that place! They were dying like rats, leaving behind pale, grief-stricken mothers in tiny farmhouses with an attic full of old toys. Whoever went over there to fight for one year would be on easy street when he came home; naturalization, work, social security, integration, medals. Everywhere there were recruitment centers. To each volunteer the country opened its heart.

Bobby and José María enlisted so they wouldn't be deported. And after three months of training at an army base they left in an enormous airplane. Life was a marvelous adventure; the trip was unforgettable. Having been born in a poor, miserable, sad country, and having known the busiest city in the world, with thousands of deprivations, it's true; but all this was behind them because now they were wearing a green uniform, flying over plains, seas, and snow-capped mountains, clutching powerful weapons and were becoming young men still filled with promise, exploring the realm of the unknown.

The laundress María has plenty of postcards of temples, markets, and exotic streets, all written in a small fastidious hand. Where could Seoul be? There are lots of ads and cabarets. Then came letters from the front lines that described to us the first attack, which forced him to take a few days off. Thanks to these documents, we were able to piece together fairly well the things that happened to him. Gradually, step by step, Bobby came closer to his rendezvous with destiny. It was necessary to reach a certain parallel and to confront a wave of yellow-skinned soldiers who descended from the northern hills like kernels of corn. For this, the volunteers, the unconquerable watchmen of the West, were there to lend a hand.

José María was saved by a miracle and proudly showed off the stump of his right arm when he returned to Lima months later. His squad had been sent to scout a rice field, where supposedly the Korean advance guard was waiting to ambush them. Bobby didn't suffer, José María said; the first blast blew his helmet off and his head rolled into a trench, all of its dyed, tangled hair hanging down. Now he had only lost an arm, but he was there, alive, telling his story, drinking cold beer, powder gone now and more zambo than ever, living comfortably off what he received as compensation for having been mutilated.

By then Roberto's mother had suffered her second attack, one which erased her from the world. She never read the official letter informing her that Bob López had died in action and was entitled to an honorable citation and remuneration for his family. No one could collect it.

Footnote

And Queca? Perhaps if Bob had known her story maybe his life would have been different or maybe it wouldn't have; no one will ever know. Billy Mulligan took her to his country, as agreed, to a town in Kentucky where his father owned a pork-canning business. They spent several months in ecstasy in that pretty house with wide sidewalks, a fence, a garden, and all the electric appliances invented by technology: in short, it was a house like a hundred thousand others in that country-continent. Gradually the Irish in him, which his Puritan upbringing had suppressed for so long, began to reveal itself; at the same time, Queca's eyes grew larger and acquired that sadness typical of the Limeños. Billy was coming home later each night; he became addicted to slot machines and car racing; his feet grew bigger and developed callouses; he discovered a malignant mole on his neck; on Saturdays he filled up on bourbon at the Kentucky Friends' Club; he had an affair with a woman employee at the firm; he wrecked the car twice; his look turned into a fixed, watery stare; and he ended up beating his wife, the pretty, unforgettable Queca, in the early hours of dawn on Sundays, while he smiled stupidly and called her a shitty half-breed.

PARIS, 1975

The Little Laid Cow

*T*he four men crossed the deserted street, entered the vestibule, climbed the stairs, and, after pushing the door open, made their way into the spacious, red-carpeted living room. For awhile no one said a word as they shuffled around in the half-dark, stumbling over one another, searching for chairs, ashtrays or simply a light switch. Bastidas turned on the crystal chandelier and, after lighting a cigarette, broke the silence with a sigh, "Well, yes, it's a real shame!"

"Especially under these circumstances," Manrique the engineer added, comfortably settling himself on the couch.

"I haven't slept a wink all night," yawned Gandolfo, idly looking at a shelf where he thought he saw a bottle.

"These mirrors!" Cantela exclaimed. "They give you the look of death. Why don't you sell them, Bastidas? They're really horrible."

"Family heirlooms," Bastidas said. "Besides, my wife would kill me. She thinks they're elegant."

"Your wife still doesn't know anything?" Manrique asked.

"Not yet," Bastidas said. "I'll tell her tomorrow when she wakes up. At noon, that is. Do you all want something to drink?"

When Bastidas stepped out of the living room, Cantela strolled about, looking at the furniture and the porcelain. "This isn't a living room; it's a museum. I'd sell everything; I'd take out this carpet which probably has centuries of dust in it and I'd put four or five modern pieces of furniture in here."

"Did you see old man Choper?" Gandolfo asked. "He was in the dining room. He drank all night long."

"He's as strong as an oak," Cantela added. "A rascal, besides."

Bastidas came back in with a bottle of rum. "You said it, a rascal. But an admirable fellow. Do you know how old he is? No one really knows. But for sure he's buried just about everyone in Tarma. And as far back as I can remember, I've always seen him with a beard, but healthy. The only one older was Cárdenas the shoe repairman and he croaked four years ago."

"Exactly what does Choper do?" Manrique asked. "I always see him roaming about the plaza."

"That old man is a night owl," Bastidas went on. "At night he doesn't even sleep: he makes love. Two years ago one of my maids got pregnant. Who did it to you? I asked her: 'Choper.' "

"I've heard that her mother cursed him," Cantela remarked, "and he dragged her by the hair through the Plaza de Armas."

"It's true," Gandolfo said. "I saw it with my own eyes. I was seven years old then and used to come to Tarma every day on the milk wagon."

"He's done worse things," Bastidas said. "My father remembered them all. When I was a young boy he would tell me about Choper's exploits; he would scare me with him when I didn't eat my soup."

"One time he strung up a bull," Cantela said. "He used to be really strong."

"But the most dreadful thing happened during election time some fifty years ago, when the Velardistas and the Rodriguistas were arguing about a delegation. Choper was on the side of the Velardistas and on voting day he rode in on a horse and stole the ballot boxes, killing a policeman. They chased him to the top of Casapalca, put five bullets in him, threw him in Lake Marcapomacocha, and cracked his forehead open with a stick so he wouldn't float to the surface. A month later he was back in Tarma and killed three Rodriguistas."

"I can't stand to see blood," Gandolfo said. "It must be horrible to bleed to death."

"A little laid cow!" the engineer Manrique said, laying his empty glass on the table.

The others emptied their glasses and laid them on the table too.

"Where did you get that expression?" Cantela asked. "It's not from around here. A little laid cow! It sounds childish."

"It's from Cuzco," Manrique said. "I worked there for two years. I heard it in a bar from a math professor."

"What time does the post office open?" Gandolfo interrupted. "I'd like to get this over with as soon as possible."

"But we haven't decided yet who's going to do the talking."

"Let's do what I said before: let's leave it to chance."

"Bring in some dice, Bastidas," Cantela said. "Or some cards. That way we'll at least have some fun."

A voice rang through the house. "Bastidas!"

"Wait, my wife's calling me. You all woke her up with your chatter. Why don't you help yourselves to another drink?"

While Bastidas was making his way toward the bedrooms, Manrique poured more drinks. "Every time he took a swig that math professor would also say: 'There's an inner voice.' I never found out why he said it. He probably didn't know himself. Each drunk does his thing."

"I had a friend," Gandolfo said, "who every time he got drunk would say 'process.' Just that one word, nothing else. He repeated it all night long, pensive, as if it were something very profound."

Bastidas reappeared.

"So, did you tell her?" Gandolfo inquired.

"Not yet; I don't want to upset her. I'll let her find out tomorrow."

"Tomorrow?" Manrique said pointing toward the window. "Tomorrow's already here."

Bastidas went to the window, pulled back the heavy drapes. A celestial light poured into the room.

"Yeah, and in a little while the post office will open. What are we going to play?"

"Poker," Manrique said. "I'm unbeatable at that."

"The winner will make the phone call," Cantela said. "Do you want that assignment?"

"Not on your life! Let's play something else then."

"Oh, life, life!" Bastidas complained, sipping his drink. "What is life? A little flame at the tip of a candle, exposed to a strong wind."

"Life's a very fragile thing," Cantela added.

"I'm fed up with philosophy," Gandolfo said. "I have to get back out to my ranch. Let's get on with it. Do you have some dice? Let's roll them. Let's play high or low. The guy who gets the lowest score loses."

"Okay," Manrique approved. "That way it'll be quicker."

Bastidas opened the drawer of a small gaming table and took out a little dice box.

"Doctor Céspedes is a good person, don't you think?" Gandolfo said. "He doesn't talk much, which is unusual. I read people by the way they laugh. He has an uninhibited laugh which seems to lay him wide open, revealing, I don't know . . . his soul."

"His nudity," Cantela added.

"Don't make jokes," Manrique said. "I wouldn't want to be in his shoes. What the hell made him take off for Lima?"

"His mother was sick," Bastidas said.

"Besides, he's not a drunk," Manrique added. "One time in Cuzco I had to see a doctor quick because I had an ingrown toenail and couldn't walk. That poor doctor was drunk as a skunk. He operated on me by candlelight because there was a power outage while I was in his office. He came close to cutting my foot off, that brute. End result: it made me grow a sixth toe. On my right foot I have six toes now. I don't know what that animal did to me."

"A graft," Gandolfo said.

"Gather around the table," Bastidas said. "But first let's drink to good health."

When everyone had drained his glass, Manrique said, "A little laid cow," and rolled his glass over the carpet.

"There's an inner voice," Gandolfo added.

"Let's play right now," Bastidas urged, jiggling the dice box. "The highest or lowest, right?"

"Let's keep it simple," Cantela said. "The one who rolls the lowest number loses."

Bastidas rolled and came up with a three. "Shit! At least the one and the two are still left."

Gandolfo rolled a six.

"See? A lucky devil when it comes to dice."

"You can go home now," Cantela said. "And sleep well."

Manrique rolled a four.

"Another set free."

"It's between Cantela and me," Bastidas said. "I knew it!"

Cantela rolled a three, the same as Bastidas.

"Didn't I tell you so? Now to break the tie."

"But first a drink," Manrique suggested. "And then to the market for a cup of hot broth."

After a toast, Bastidas rolled the dice and again came up with a three. Cantela rolled and got a six.

"Ah, life, life, life!" Bastidas sighed. "I always get the raw deal. Now to resign myself to it."

"Do you think that they've opened yet?" Gandolfo asked. "I'm dying to get some sleep. I'll go to the post office with you for solidarity. I wonder how the hell my cows are doing."

"Cows! I'll bet you've never squeezed an udder," Bastidas said. "You know as much about cows as people who've seen pictures of them on packs of butter."

"That's why I have my Indians," Gandolfo said. "To me a cow is only so much money a day. What about you? Have you ever castrated a ram?"

"I've not only slaughtered them but eaten them, too. I've even eaten the mountain oysters. Can't you see I even have the face of a ram?"

"Come on, let's get going," Cantela said. "I have to open my drugstore at seven."

"Aren't we going to do one more little laid cow?" Manrique asked.

"The last one," Bastidas agreed as he filled the glasses. "I have to muster up enough courage so I can sound like a gentleman."

"What are you going to say to him?" Gandolfo asked. "I'd be hard pressed for words."

"I'll think of something," Bastidas said. "To your health!"

After making the last toast, the four men left the living room, went downstairs, and found themselves on Lima Street. There wasn't one car at that hour as they walked down the middle of the road, crossed Mantarana ditch and came to the post office. The door was locked.

"Doesn't anyone ever work around here?" Bastidas protested. "It's already after seven."

"Let's walk around the plaza," Cantela suggested. "That way I can take a quick look at my store."

They strolled awhile through the small square shaded by mountain palm trees. The cathedral bells began to toll.

"Do you know that they invite the choir members to have pastry and beer after singing?" Bastidas said. "They leave a basket there in the belfry, behind the door leading to the choir loft. When I was a boy I went up to the tower with my brother Jacinto during Mass; we drank up all the beer and pissed in the bottles. I never found out what happened afterward."

"Eight o'clock," Cantela said. "I'm going to the drugstore. Don't you see a fellow standing over there? He must be a customer . . ."

"You're coming with us," Gandolfo said, grabbing him by the arm. "Don't run out on us. Bastidas is going to do the talking but we have to be at his side."

The four men locked arms and headed for the post office.

"I have to make a call to Lima," Bastidas told the employee. "Give me the telephone directory."

After leafing through the letter C section, he told her to connect him with 58666.

"Go to the first booth," the woman said. "I'll signal you when to pick up the receiver."

The four moved toward the booth.

"We all can't go in," Bastidas said. "At least one of you stay beside me."

"You're pale, Bastidas!" Gandolfo said. "Now you really do look like a sheep."

"It's best to leave the door open," Cantela said. "The three of us will stand in the door like only one man."

"All for one and one for all." Manrique yawned.

"You can speak now!" the employee shouted.

Bastidas unhooked the receiver while his three friends gathered at the door.

"Light me a cigarette," Bastidas told his friends. "Alo? Is this the Céspedes residence? Yes, a call from Tarma. With Doctor Herminio Céspedes, please." To his friends, "They're going to wake him!"

"What's making your hands shake like that?" Cantela said. "Come on, take a puff of the cigarette and remember our bullfighting days on the ranch. Do you all know that Bastidas was a terrific bullfighter?"

"Of course," Gandolfo said. "When we were fifteen years old . . ."

"Shut up!" Bastidas ordered. "Alo? With Doctor Céspedes? From Tarma. This is Bastidas speaking . . ."

There was total silence. The three friends watched Bastidas' face.

"It's something very serious . . . Your wife . . ."

Bastidas put his hand over the receiver. To his friends, "He's asking me if she's given birth! What do I tell him?"

Cantela made an impatient gesture. Manrique anxiously looked away toward the street.

"A little laid cow," whispered Gandolfo.

"No, Doctor," Bastidas continued. "It's something very painful. Your wife died last night from a hemorrhage . . . It was a premature delivery. The child too . . . We . . . your friends in Tarma . . . well . . . we wanted to tell you . . . we want to offer . . ."

"Don't stammer for God's sake!" Cantela protested.

Bastidas put his hand over the receiver, "But what do you want me to say? He's crying!"

Stretching the earpiece toward them, he passed it around and made each of them listen.

"The best thing is to hang up," Gandolfo said.

"Alo?" Bastidas continued. "Can you hear me, Doctor Céspedes? Alo? Gotta go!" and he hung up.

The four men walked silently toward the door.

"Put the call on my bill," Bastidas told the telephone operator.

In the street they felt a little relieved as they breathed the morning air.

"Let's go to the market for breakfast," Manrique suggested.

"Yes," Bastidas said, leading the way. "Do you know they made me grand marshal of the Santa Ana Fair?"

When they got to Sequialta, Gandolfo took out running and gave a grandiose kick to an empty can of Gloria milk.

"A little laid cow!" Manrique shouted.

The four men broke into laughter.

PARIS, 1961

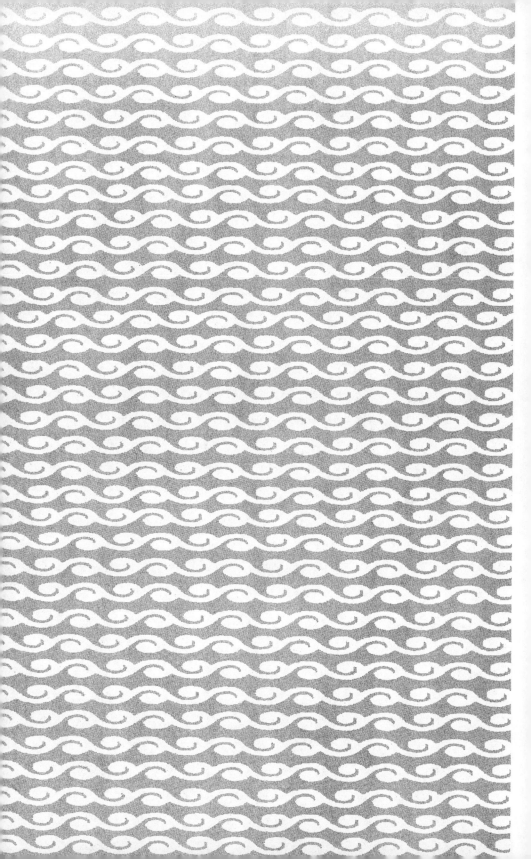

The Jacaranda Trees

*T*he house was there intact, with its high adobe wall facing the Avenida de los Jacarandas. He had come on foot from the Plaza de Armas with his valise in hand, remembering what he had read one time about perfect cities, the kind one can stroll across from one end to the other in a quarter of an hour. Everything was the same: the guava trees in the garden, the three eucalyptus, and even the rooms in which he found the same old disorder. He drifted through them until nightfall, surrounded by silent voices and even silent music coming from the Victrola where the record was still poised with the needle stuck on the last groove.

"I've done the right thing by coming," Olga said. "The house is so near the office. That way, when I feel lonely, I can get out and come visit you."

Lorenzo observed the bed, covered by a native blanket with geometrical designs, and he thought he saw a clenched hand on the polychrome cloth. Then he picked up the tourist guidebook on the night table and went out onto the Avenida de los Jacarandas.

He didn't go toward the Spanish Arch, where the city came to an end along the river and pasture lands, but rather headed downtown. The 28 de Julio Street was deserted at that hour. The villagers were having supper and the outsiders, incapable of accustoming themselves to so many belfries and to so little recreation, were drinking at bars or watching a western film at the only movie theater. Lorenzo passed in front of the university rector's old mansion, the most beautiful house in the city with its gray stone portico and its colonial door. Further on, he stopped in front of Santa Ana Church and observed its facade.

"Look at that elephant," Olga said. "There beside the apostles. What can it mean?"

No one could ever explain why the anonymous stonecutter who carved the facade positioned that animal beside the sacred figures.

He was already at the Plaza de Armas. Only one person was walking by at that hour: the rector. Smoking his pipe, he was taking his ten nightly turns around the plaza adorned with mountain palms. Lorenzo approached him.

"I'm glad you've returned, Doctor Manrique, but I'm sorry you don't plan to stay. The students were so happy with you. And how are your affairs going?"

"I'll take care of them tomorrow. If there aren't any problems, I'll leave Saturday on the first plane."

"This afternoon Miss Evans came to see me," the rector continued. "I hope she adapts. It would be helpful if you'd talk a little with her, before turning your job over to her."

"We were on the same plane this morning, but I hardly spoke to her. I promised her my guidebook to the city."

Miss Evans had screamed that morning when the twin-engine plane, after circling over the cloudy sky for a quarter of an hour, suddenly dove through a clearing looking for the airport.

"Don't be afraid," Lorenzo said. "These pilots are very reliable. When they know they can't land, they return to Lima."

By then Miss Evans was busy admiring the roofs of the city and its thirty-seven churches as the plane tilted one wing, giving her a bird's-eye view of them.

"What does Ayacucho mean?" she asked.

"The Place of the Dead."

The rector had finished his tenth turn. "Come by the house tomorrow evening," he said. "Come for dinner."

Lorenzo bid him good-bye and started for the tourist hotel which, although still unfinished, was occupied as rooms were added. Miss Evans was just then in the doorway, talking with the doorman.

"For dining, the Baccará, Señorita. The second street on the right."

She was wearing pants and over her shoulders she had thrown a ridiculous, unauthentic little poncho, mass-produced in the capital.

"I have the guidebook here for you," Lorenzo said. "It's not much more than a brochure, but maybe it will be useful."

He accompanied her for awhile along the Plaza de Armas. "What a difference from the coast," Miss Evans said. "Here you really breathe dry air. And have you seen the sky? I've never seen so many stars all at once."

The lobby of the movie theater lit up and a talkative population emerged, pouring into the plaza to the sound of a noisy *guaracha*.

"You're not coming along to eat?"

"No. Look. There's the restaurant."

When he was returning home under the archway of the prefecture, Ichikawa stepped out of the entrance of his department store.

"All set, professor. I spoke by radio with the company. There's no problem. You can fly out on Saturday."

Lorenzo avoided 28 de Julio Street by which the rector was returning to his residence and instead took an uphill street running parallel. It was not paved and the only light was that of the starry sky. In one of those old, neglected houses, four hundred years old and almost falling down, lived the rebel Francisco de Carbajal, decapitated by order of the Peacemaker La Gasca.

"It seems as though I've gone back several centuries in time," Olga said. "Nothing has changed here. I'm happy, Lorenzo. But these walks tire me."

He had made notes in a little book of all he had to do. His mind had begun to wander and he was forgetting everything. Earlier he had gone to see the owner of the house.

"I thought you weren't coming back from Lima, Professor Manrique. So many people are wanting me to rent them the house! Professor Manrique isn't coming back, they told me."

Lorenzo paid him for the two consecutive months he was gone and promised to turn in the keys on Saturday, before his departure.

"You know? They've criticized Doctor Alipio a lot. What people say about him! A big talker, but no intelligence."

Lorenzo hesitated, not knowing which way to go; finally he went to see the mayor. All he found was his secretary playing cards with a friend. On the office table was a decanter for rum and a skillet with cracklings.

"Ah, I don't know anything about that, professor. The mayor does, but he doesn't come by here often. Look for him at his house or at the Santa Ana Guild. Better yet, talk with the judge."

Lorenzo had forgotten the local customs. One lived according to an old, enigmatic order plagued with peculiar habits. The doctor would pick up travelers at the airport in his motor van, the mayor played the drum in processions, the deacon cured sties and ingrown nails, the bishop left with an easel on Sundays to paint the countryside, the shopkeeper Ichikawa was the radiotelegrapher and agent for the aviation company, Doctor Flores, professor of zootechnics, sang boleros on the local station, and the rector of the university had once been captain of a merchant ship.

"Viva el Peru!"

From the Hotel Sucre bar, in the shade of the portico, emerged a squalid subject wearing a hat who was being carried on the shoulders of two half-breeds. Lorenzo lowered himself onto a bench in the Plaza de Armas, watched Judge Logrono greet the passers-by while he was going toward his office being carried by his secretaries. Looking at the cathedral towers, he saw a rooster peek through the window of one of the belfries, spread his wings, and let out a shrill cock-a-doodle-doo.

"Someone lives in that tower," Olga said. "Sometimes I've seen them hang clothes out to dry."

Lorenzo immediately stood up and trailed after the judge who, upon reaching his office, got down off the shoulders of his assistants, buttoned his coat, took off his hat, and made an effort to cross the threshold of the law court with dignity.

When the professor entered his law office, he found the judge regaining his composure in front of a cup of coffee.

"On this matter here there are neither precedents nor jurisprudence," he said. "You'd best see the mayor or the court clerk Manzanares. Besides, they have to give you a certificate."

When he returned to the Plaza de Armas to go to the clerk's office, students and professors were coming out of the university to take a break and have some refreshments at the entrance. Lorenzo avoided them by taking a narrow street that went down into the tanners' district. The doorways of the old colonial mansions were now occupied by small artisans who stubbornly attempted to perpetuate, rather hopelessly, baroque crafts whose primary themes were churches, retables, and bulls. Lorenzo saw a woman coming from the district below, undulating beneath the solar glare. For awhile the sight confused him until he recognized Miss Evans coming toward him, with a camera hanging from one shoulder. She greeted him with a smile.

"Have you met your students yet?"

"I have my first class this afternoon, Doctor Manrique. The rector is going to introduce me. What poverty there is down there! Those houses really stink!"

They walked together back to the Plaza de Armas.

"At the tourist hotel there's no hot water. Last night I had to shower in ice-cold water. And they don't serve any meals; I had to go out for breakfast."

"In spite of that, you'll end up liking the city," Lorenzo said.

"Why did you quit your job then?"

"For personal reasons. But it's a city where, with a little effort, Miss Evans, one can really find happiness."

He left Miss Evans, full of more questions, in the middle of the plaza and headed for the court clerk's office. The clerk Manzanares told him he needed two witnesses, a certificate from the registrar's office, and authorization from the judge. Lorenzo left to have lunch in the upper district at an inn where only the muleteers and street-porters ate. On the road he saw an old man carrying a small, dead cow on his shoulders, and further on two barefooted, native children who were kicking the air, playing soccer with an enormous blue butterfly.

"Come closer," Olga said. "Put your ear here to my stomach. Don't you hear something? A little lower. Listen carefully. It's moving."

He had also forgotten that it was a clergyman's city. On his afternoon errands he met up with Salas the canon, picking his hairy ear with a match stick, with Monseigneur Lituma returning from his farm with a bundle of onions in his hand, with priests Huari, Lezcano, and Torrejón, and with twelve seminarists coming back from playing a game of football at the public school. By dusk he only needed to get the witnesses and to locate Doctor Alipio, who had left that morning for the country to perform an urgent operation.

He found the doctor in the waiting room of his office just as he was putting a tumor he had extracted that morning in the wide-mouthed pitcher filled with formaldehyde, the same pitcher he at first had mistaken for a fish bowl full of rare species.

"Eight kilos," he said. "The donor's name is Petronila Canas and she's forty-two years old. Within a week she'll be on her feet again and hard at work."

"I'm sorry to bother you, but you are the only one here with a van. I wanted . . ."

"At your service, professor. For you, anything. Tomorrow at six o'clock I'll come by the Avenida de los Jacarandas."

The gate to the rectory was ajar. A road made of irregular flagstones split the shady garden and led directly from the main entrance to the front steps of the mansion. Lorenzo eluded the offices, now closed, and stopped, facing the hall door, also slightly open. He rang the bell to announce himself and went in. The rector was standing beside the small portable bar, wearing a marbled jacket and a silk scarf. "Whiskey or a *pisco*?"

Lorenzo served himself a whiskey.

"The university is like a boat run aground between turbid, dry hills," the rector said. "And the city itself is like a ship stuck on a bare, God-forsaken reef. It would be difficult to put it afloat again, Doctor Manrique."

While the rector rambled on and on, Lorenzo observed the comfort of the old house, its invulnerable walls and the almost musical distribution of its space, beginning with the large parlor, followed by a series of symmetrical rooms that united around the interior cloister.

"The landowners are against me," the rector was saying. "The university scares them. They see people who used to be their servants turned into students. To them the university is a form of subversion. And if that's true, all the better."

The doorbell interrupted him just as he was beginning to berate Monseigneur Lituma on the matter of the wall separating the cathedral from the university.

"I have other guests," he said going toward the door.

Miss Evans appeared with a geranium in her hand. "Forgive me, Doctor, but it seemed so big, so clean. I picked it in the front garden. In Lima they're full of dust."

"They say that the Marquís de la Feria planted them three hundred years ago," the rector said. "The jacarandas on the avenue, too. Haven't you seen them? But, it's a lie, of course. The only thing the marquis did was to build this house."

"How's your class?" Lorenzo asked.

Miss Evans took off her coat, poured herself a whiskey that the rector offered, and sat down on a cushion on the floor, beside the fire. "There will be plenty of work. The level of the students is a bit low."

The doorbell rang again and two extremely robust young men appeared, generously greeting everyone from the doorway with wide-open arms. The view of Miss Evans, who had stretched out her legs and lifted her skirt a little to warm herself by the fire, immediately transformed them into two imperious roosters. García, with swaying hips, strutted through the hall while Sepúlveda firmly brandished his glass in his hand like an Olympic torch and, not knowing what to say, stuck out his chin and emphatically looked at his interlocutors.

Lorenzo sank down in an armchair and quietly watched the logs being consumed by the fire. A native butler wearing a white coat and white gloves appeared with a tray and served appetizers. The rector poured the whiskey while García, rejecting any attention, glued himself to the floor beside Miss Evans.

"Ayacucho is a first-rate city, Miss. Good climate, parades, everything cheap. And dances too, for those familiar with them. My friend and I are gym teachers at the university. You just take along something to drink and it's party time till dawn."

The butler signaled and the rector left his glass on the bar. "We're ready to eat."

The table was set in one of the arcades of the cloister. The rector was used to serving a French wine that he had discovered in Ichikawa's store. García, ripe with Gallic furor, at that moment invited Miss Evans to visit the gymnasium, while Sepúlveda showed the rector how to breathe after a vigorous exercise in order to avoid palpitations. Lorenzo saw a sad screen of invincible boredom drop before his eyes.

"Is it true you're returning to Lima on Saturday?" Miss Evans asked him from the opposite end of the table.

Lorenzo made out her face, it became a blur, then he saw it again clearly and finally he was able to say, "Day after tomorrow. I've only come to . . ."

He was interrupted. The rector cleared his throat.

" . . . attend to some business."

During the rest of the meal he hardly spoke, restricting himself to distractedly listening to the rector tell Miss Evans the history of the university, the biographies of its principal dignitaries, the avatars for the opening and closing ceremonies for the past three centuries; in the meantime García and Sepúlveda were losing their voices in a banal discussion about acrobatics.

"Let's have our coffee in the parlor," the rector said.

Lorenzo relaxed again in his armchair and lit a cigarette. After coffee, the rector served a blessed *pisco* made by the Redemptorist priests of Huanta and put a record of Ayacucho music on the Victrola. Sepúlveda went up to the former marine to tell him about the film he had seen the day before—*Dracula and the Spiderman*—while García, taking out a white handkerchief, offered to show Miss Evans some *huayno* dance steps.

"Please excuse me," Lorenzo said, standing up. "Tomorrow's going to be hectic for me. Will you all be at the gym in the morning? I'll come by there. I have to ask you a favor."

"Anything. Just name it," Sepúlveda responded.

He woke up late from a night full of dreams about which his memory only held traces: a Gothic abbey, a reddish, autumnal forest, a serpent. He ate breakfast in the bar near the entrance and headed for the gym. Sepúlveda, in white flannel pants, was entertaining himself on the parallel bars while García, in black mesh, was doing somersaults on an exercise mat in front of his students.

Lorenzo took them to a corner. "I need you to serve as witnesses this afternoon."

"Delighted, Professor. For a marriage?"

García immediately intervened. "Don't pay any attention to him, Professor. It's just that Sepúlveda has fallen for the little English lady. He doesn't know what he's saying anymore. It's all set, then. Come by for us at six o'clock."

When Lorenzo left, García called after him, "Last night we accompanied her to her hotel. She told us that she had taken ballet as a girl."

In the Plaza de Armas he stood blinking, blinded by the morning sun. He saw Salas the canon leave the cathedral carrying an image of the Immaculate Conception by its waist; he saw the priests Huari, Lezcano, and Torrejón coming out of the Baccará Restaurant with their hands folded across their bellies. A group of natives suddenly emerged from the lower district on their way to the market, carrying enormous blocks of salt strapped on their backs.

"Look at my feet," Olga said. "They're swollen. I don't want to be taken care of here. How can a city like this, where they don't even know about the wheel, have a good doctor? Take me to Lima two months ahead of time."

He was awakened from his nap by the sound of a car horn. He walked across the garden with images of the burdened Indians, the explosion of rain that afternoon, the bottle of wine that he downed before falling asleep still in his memory. When he opened the door he clearly saw Doctor Alipio seated at the steering wheel of his Chevrolet van.

"Look at the jacarandas," he said. "The cloudburst has rejuvenated them. A week from now they'll be in bloom. It's six o'clock sharp, Professor. I kept my word."

Lorenzo went back into the house. He washed his face with cold water, meticulously combed his hair, and, after putting on a coat and tie, went out again.

"We have to go by the gym. Sepúlveda and García are waiting for me."

"Witnesses?"

"Very strong ones."

The van made its way to the Plaza de Armas, picked up the acrobats and took the road to the cemetery. Manzanares, the notary, was waiting for them at the gate.

The five began to walk between the graves guided by the caretaker. A late afternoon sun in a clear sky was lighting up the pampas of Ayacucho to the east.

"The rector wants to build a monument to the battle," Alipio said.

"Here it is," the caretaker said.

It was the place where the dead were put in superimposed niches. The caretaker chiseled the outer slab of the tombstone, pulling it out with a tug, exposing one end of the coffin.

"Our turn," Sepúlveda said, grabbing the coffin by its iron handles.

"If you'll allow me," said the notary. "Some signatures here."

After signing the exhumation certificate, Sepúlveda pulled on the iron ring and with García's help extracted the large box. Alipio and Lorenzo lent a shoulder and between the four of them they carried the coffin to the gate and put it in the van.

"A sad thing," García said. "When one thinks! Señora Olga liked cracklings so very much."

"To Ichikawa's place?" asked Doctor Alipio.

"No, home." Lorenzo said. "He told me that tomorrow the truck would come by to take us to the airport."

It was getting dark on the Avenida de los Jacarandas. They left the coffin in the center of the shadowed room. Lorenzo was silent, surrounded by coughing, hoarse shadows, trying in vain to remember where the light switch was located.

"We'll leave you," García said finally. "You'll still have some things to do before your departure. It's been a pleasure."

"I don't feel well," Olga said. "I feel a heaviness here in my chest. I can't breathe well. Put on the Vivaldi record again, please."

When night fell he went out again. He walked the entire Avenida de los Jacarandas to the Spanish Arch, crossed the fields, reached the border of the river, returned by way of the Convent of the Clare nuns, and, despite the gusty wind that blew up, he continued his walk through the higher neighborhoods with their little streets muddied by the afternoon showers. Coming down toward the Plaza de Armas, he saw the rector who, dissuaded by the wind, seemed to be returning to his mansion without having taken his ten turns. The movie theater advertising the revival of the Dracula movie, was absorbing a procession of hunched over, tenacious insomniacs. He only needed to see the bell towers of Santo Domingo and to get there he passed in front of the tourist hotel. After seeing them from the front and the side, he stopped, hoping the biting wind coming down out of the high district with less and less force, would altogether subside. In the enigmatic window of the cathedral tower, a pair of men's drawers fluttered, then assumed a rigid, cubist form.

Turning around, he saw Miss Evans leaving the hotel and coming straight toward him, bouncing along as she buttoned her raincoat. "I'm going to an engagement party. Your friends the athletes invited me last night. What's that like? It will be at Bendezú's place."

Lorenzo half closed his eyes a moment as if searching within himself for something lost and then opened them.

"That's near the post office," he said. "I'll accompany you a ways; it will give me the chance to say good-bye to a little more of Ayacucho. Tomorrow I return to Lima."

"Why do you like Ayacucho so much? It's a city without a countryside. They say that to see trees you must go as far as Huanta. Tomorrow I'll visit it."

"I think I've already told you once. Because here it doesn't take much to be happy."

"And what have you come to do this time? The rector told me you should stay, that he would divide the English class. You could teach one group and I the other."

"Careful!"

Miss Evans gave a quick jump in order to avoid a puddle of water.

"You've obviously studied ballet."

"Who told you?"

"Your friends. But I already knew that. I've known it for a very long time."

They were already in front of Bendezú's house. Through the entrance, an opening in a high adobe wall, one could hear the rhythm of a cha-cha-cha. Miss Evans was quiet, scrutinizing him in the dark, clutching her patent leather purse in her hands.

"Aren't you going in?"

"No."

Again he was awakened that Saturday morning, not by the car horn, but rather by a steady, firm pounding on the screen door to the living room. Through the glass Lorenzo saw Ichikawa, who, after having pushed open the gate and crossed the garden, was noisily approaching the edge of his dream.

"The flight's canceled, Professor. I spoke by radio with someone in Lima. It's overcast there and they can't take off. It's not clear here either. The plane isn't coming in till Monday."

Lorenzo, tying his robe, looked around bewildered. He saw the coffin.

"Excuse me for waking you, but I came early to notify you."

Since Lorenzo wasn't saying anything, Ichikawa looked at the coffin, too, and took off his hat. "I want to express my condolences again, Doctor. These things happen in life."

Lorenzo started toward the door and opened it. "I hope you're right about Monday. I don't have anything to do here anymore."

"I understand, Doctor."

Before leaving, Ichikawa hesitated a moment. "Is it true what they say about Doctor Alipio? They say he didn't want to come, that he was at a dinner."

"It's a lie," Lorenzo responded, closing the door.

The bier was still in the middle of the room. He pushed it toward the wall and stepped back a little to examine it. He went back to it and covered it with the three ponchos that he had bought for a pittance from the *campesinos* who went from door to door. Contemplating the gardens, he saw appearing among the *guayabos*, behind the fence, the lush, yet foreboding top of a jacaranda tree.

Then he made himself some coffee, shaved, and quickly set out for the Plaza de Armas. The bus to Huanta was about to leave. Behind Father Torrejón and three Redemptorist priests, he saw her.

"What? I thought you would be flying toward Lima by now."

"A last-minute delay, Miss Evans. I'm leaving on Monday. I want a closer look at the countryside."

The bus left the city behind within five minutes and penetrated the landscape that the rector had defined forever as hills, turbulent and dry. Armies of spiny plants—cacti, prickly pears, magueys—were descending from the craggy places to the edge of the highway.

"Yesterday at the party I found out something."

"How did the engagement party go?"

"I left early. Everybody was getting drunk. I didn't know you were a widower."

"What else did your friends tell you?"

"That your wife is buried here."

Lorenzo was quiet, looking through the window. They kept descending toward the Huanta valley.

"It's a topic that I prefer not to discuss," he said when the first orange groves appeared.

The bus stopped at a hamlet to pick up a group of natives.

"Let's get off here," Lorenzo said. "There's practically nothing to see in Huanta."

In a second they were in the dirt street seeing the bus move away, its tires sinking into a muddy rut. After crossing a stretch of thickets and dwarf trees, they came to a murky river, strewn with litter. They looked at it for a moment without saying a word.

"The truth is, the countryside really bores me," Lorenzo said. "I'm a city boy. Shall we go back?"

Again on the highway they waited for the bus in vain, a truck that would take them back to Ayacucho. Miss Evans alluded to some sandwiches that she had forgotten at the hotel; then Lorenzo suggested they go into one of the roadside inns. They were promised steak with fried eggs and for starters two enormous bottles of beer were placed in front of them. The beer was warm. Miss Evans, putting her hand to a lock of hair on her forehead, trapped a fly.

"I'm constantly thinking about the Mandrake Club," Lorenzo said. "When I lived in London I became a member for two pounds sterling. In the evenings I would go by there for spaghetti and a game of chess."

Lorenzo measured the silence following that statement; he noted that it was unbearably drawn out, so much so that his head filled with a spontaneous humming that couldn't be coming from outside himself, but rather from his anxiety.

"You have never told me what you did as a boy when you lived in London," Olga said. "Who did you run around with? Did you have a girlfriend?"

"I know it," Miss Evans added. "It's in Soho, near the Turkish baths."

"Didn't we dance there one night in the dance hall next to the bar? Just before Christmas?"

"They were playing a New Orleans piece, something by Sydney Bechet if I'm not mistaken, an extremely mellow thing called 'Absent-Minded Blues.' "

"But then you called yourself Winnie. And you were a nurse. A redhead."

"I still call myself Winnie. That's my middle name. Vivien Winnie Evans. As for the color of my hair . . ."

Lorenzo observed Miss Evans with her tiny dark freckles on skin so white that the rector would describe it for sure as cerulean or alabastrine; then he began to laugh so hard that he got her laughing and not only her, but a group of truck drivers who were eating at the next table. The innkeeper was also laughing as he brought the steaks topped with eggs. Lorenzo noticed that a fly had landed on his egg, and stopped laughing. The torrid beer he had drunk was coming back into his mouth.

"You could say it's a farce," he said. "But, why can't it be true?"

"I can give you more details," Miss Evans added, smiling. "I clearly remember many things. What painting was behind the counter, above the mirror?"

Lorenzo hesitated. "It's useless playing these games."

"Why?"

"We believe we frequent the same places, Miss Evans, that we encounter the same people. But it's an illusion. We simply pass nearby. If life is a road—like they usually say it is—it's neither straight nor curved. Let's say it's a spiral."

"Where does it lead?"

"To the place of the dead."

The innkeeper came up to see if they wanted anything else, but Lorenzo asked for the bill. They were again out on the road, looking at the sky that had cleared, and waiting for the bus. Miss Evans went over to the edge of a brook to break off a slender branch of Spanish broom. Lorenzo observed her from afar, watching her bend her knees and lean over.

"No, Miss Evans!" he shouted. "You're not Winnie! Winnie was an English girl that I met seven years ago at the Mandrake Club and she was also my wife, the one who died from a heart attack two months ago, when she was expecting a baby!"

Miss Evans was looking at him very seriously now. In the distance, standing erect on her long legs, she kept looking at him while she clasped the Spanish broom against her chest. She began walking toward him, smiling.

"The last thing you said is a lie," she said. "Winnie was not your wife," and taking him by the chin she pulled him toward her until she felt his mouth.

When they returned, the jacarandas were glistening under the late afternoon sun. Lorenzo pushed open the door to his room and one by one opened the windows facing the garden.

"I'm hungry," Miss Evans said, sitting on the bed with the polychrome quilt.

Lorenzo went into the kitchen and found only half a bottle of an old conventual *pisco* and a piece of Bologne sausage. When he went back to the room with a bottle, he saw that Miss Evans was just about to pick up the arm of the record player.

"Don't touch that, please."

Miss Evans obeyed, returning to the bed, and Lorenzo, with the bottle in his hand, saw the coffin covered with the three ponchos while he was looking for a place to sit down. Then he closed the window curtains and sat down on an easy chair made of wood from the colonies.

"I don't know if you were aware of it," Miss Evans said, "but when we boarded the plane my seat happened to be next to a priest. Then, before we took off, I came and sat next to you."

Lorenzo took a sip of *pisco*.

"I wasn't aware of anything, Miss Evans."

"And you didn't talk to me during the entire trip, except just before landing in Ayacucho, when the plane seemed to be dropping because of an air pocket. Why did you offer me your guidebook?"

"Because at the airport terminal in Lima, before they called the passengers, I realized that, yes, now I know, I realized that Winnie was among us again."

Miss Evans broke into laughter. "Offer me a little of that. Here you go with your stories again."

Lorenzo passed the bottle to Miss Evans and returned to his easy chair. It was growing dark. They were silent. Again the voice was trying hard to penetrate his ears. Lorenzo cleared his throat several times, trying to silence it.

"Put on the Vivaldi record again please. And go look for Doctor Alipio. Go, Lorenzo, right now, I beg you."

Getting to his feet, he went over to the record player, turned it on, and lifted the needle. "It can't be; it can't be!"

"What?" Miss Evans asked.

Vivaldi's *Four Seasons* began to play very softly.

"I want to sort all this out. I have to remember things well . . . I want to know why I waited so long to go look for him when she asked me to. I thought it was just a whim; she'd felt bad so many times and things like that happen to women, even more so when they're expecting."

"I don't understand, Doctor Manrique."

"It was raining, so I picked up the umbrella. I was making a list of the books that I was thinking about ordering from Lima, a very long list; I couldn't remember some of the authors. I was lazy, besides. It's true that Doctor Alipio was delayed because of a dinner, one of those local affairs you're familiar with now—a bottle of *pisco* and a plate of cracklings for every guest and speeches, interminable speeches. But I took even longer in going to look for him."

"So when you returned?"

"The Vivaldi record was over."

"And Winnie?"

"Winnie? You mean Olga, Miss Evans. Winnie was the English girl. Olga had fallen asleep like a little bird, with her head tucked under an arm and her hand curled up, the hand that reached for me, waited for me, and, not finding me, curled itself into a little ball over the quilt where you're sitting. She and the other life she was carrying inside were asleep. Like they say, asleep forever. Make no mistake, forever."

"Take it easy," Miss Evans said. "Look." In the semidarkness she was handing him the bottle.

Lorenzo drew near her and, when he reached for the neck of the bottle, she took his arm.

"Sit here. What you're telling me is terrible. Your friends told me that she had died, but I didn't know how or any details; I don't know how to console someone, I've never known how. Forgive me?"

"Love," Lorenzo said, "is as bitter as death; this is something I read one time on a tombstone in the English cemetery of Nice."

Miss Evans was quiet. Lorenzo was holding her hand tightly. In the silence, in the darkness, Lorenzo could hear only his own panting, a breath that took the form of another body, as if it belonged to another man, but was coming from his own mouth.

"And the worst thing of all is that I want you, Miss Evans. I want you badly. A crazy desire to . . . right here, right now . . ."

"Who?"

"Winnie. Yes, I want Winnie, in front of the other Winnie."

"Which Winnie?"

"The one over there."

Miss Evans looked at the ponchos which formed a shadow even darker than the darkness itself. The remaining daylight was disappearing, leaving behind a rectangular form.

"All this is crazy," she said, pulling away from Lorenzo, who was brusquely trying to nuzzle her neck with his lips. "It's a macabre joke, Professor Manrique. I'm sorry, but I don't want any part of this game. Besides, I have to go."

Lorenzo pulled back at once, letting her stand up and look for her purse in the dark. The *Four Seasons* could scarcely be heard. Then he saw her start for the door.

"Let me accompany you."

Together they crossed the garden with the eucalyptus trees and came to the gate. Miss Evans suddenly stopped. Her hands were clutching her purse.

"I hope you have a good trip, Doctor. Believe me . . ."

Stopping herself, she turned her back and began to walk away. Lorenzo paused for a moment, copiously and anxiously breathing the perfumed air of the jacarandas. Seeing her from some twenty feet away, he opened his mouth, "Miss Evans!"

Miss Evans kept on walking.

"Winnie!"

She kept moving away.

"Olga!"

Now, slowing down, she stopped, without turning around.

Lorenzo moved toward her, faster and faster, and just as he reached her he saw her turn around with her hair flowing, a freckled, youthful redhead, smiling, with her relaxed arms outstretched.

"Olga," he repeated. "Can this be possible? Again!"

He hugged her, kissing her so hard that they lost their balance and toppled against the wall. Finally, taking her by the waist, he turned her around, pulled her close, and led her toward the house. In the stillness of the night Miss Evans allowed herself to be swept along as she gazed at the breathing trees.

"What did the rector say they're called?"

"Jacaranda trees. Again, Olga, we're strolling under the jacarandas."

They studied them for a moment. Lorenzo smiled.

"What is it?" asked Miss Evans.

"I was thinking about what the epitaph said. Even the English can make mistakes."

PARIS, 1970

Bottles and Men

~~~~~~~~~~~~

"They're looking for you," the porter said. "A man is waiting for you at the entrance."

Luciano finished with a powerful return, making his opponent shrink back. Then, leaving his racket on the bench, he started down the narrow dirt path. At first he saw a bald pate, then a poorly covered paunch, but it was not until he got close enough to make out the rough, Javanese masklike face that he felt his knees go weak. Since there was a bar just before the exit, he edged his way toward it and ordered a beer.

After taking the first sip, his lips still burning with shame, he looked toward the fence. The man was still standing there, now and then casting timid looks inside the club. Occasionally, he would observe his hands with the ingenuous attention that people accustomed to waiting often give the most insignificant things.

Luciano swigged down his beer and boldly started toward the gate. When the man saw him, he stiffened and looked at him with amazement. Soon he regained his composure, took a dirty hand from his pocket, and extended it. "Give me some change," he said. "I need to go to Callao."

Luciano didn't respond; he hadn't seen his father for eight years. His eyes could not stop looking at those features that he had known so well as a child and that were appearing now completely worn and wrinkled by time.

"Didn't you hear what I said?" he repeated. "I need you to give me some change."

"That's no way to greet me," Luciano said. "Follow me."

As he walked, he could hear hurried footsteps behind him and then felt a hand grab him by the arm."

"I'm sorry, Ñato![1] It's just that I'm washed up, no money, no job . . . I came up from Arequipa two days ago."

Luciano kept on walking. "And what about all these years?"

"I've been in Chile, in Argentina . . ."

"Did things go okay?"

"Never better! I lived the grand life."

1. The word *ñato* means pug-nosed. Peruvians often use such words to express their affection toward family members or close friends.

When they reached the bar, Luciano ordered two beers.

"No beer for me! I'm a *pisco* man myself. I'll have a Soldeíca.[2] "I asked about you and they told me you were still at the club."

It was hot. They could only hear the sound of the rackets hitting the balls out on the spacious playing surface. Luciano looked toward the court where his tennis partner was waiting for him, fingering the net and looking bored. He thought the guy might walk into the bar and create an embarrassing situation.

"Were you playing?" the old man asked. "You can go ahead with your game. I'll down this and take off. I didn't come to chat. But you've got to leave me some change for the streetcar. I've got to go out to the wharf to look for a job."

"I've got plenty of time," Luciano replied as he looked toward the counter again. His father raised the glass to his lips, took the first sip, and quickly wiped his mouth with his hand, copying that gesture from the local drinkers in the taverns of the district. They both were quiet, sitting close to one another, irreparably separated by years of absence. The old man turned his eyes in the direction of the club's facilities, toward the beautiful building hidden behind a grove of trees.

"All this is new; I've never seen it! I remember when I was a janitor and we lived over there, in that little house. You've come up in the world; you don't just pick up balls anymore. You mix with the high society."

"I haven't retrieved balls in years."

"Now you play the game!" the old man sighed.

Luciano started to feel uncomfortable. The bartender couldn't keep his eyes off that strange visitor with the greasy shirt and poorly shaven chin. Men of that sort only came into the club through the back door, when there was a clogged drain pipe.

"Here comes your rival!" his father said, tossing down his drink. "I'm leaving. Give me what I came for."

Luciano saw his tennis partner striding toward him, hitting invisible balls with his racket. Reaching into his pocket, he anxiously searched for some coins, and for a moment held them hostage in his hand, before finally letting them go.

"Take your time," he said. "No one rushes me."

His friend stopped in front of the bar. "Are you coming or not? I'm beginning to cool down."

"I'd like you to meet my father," Luciano said.

"Your father?"

2. A brand of liquor.

They shook hands. While they were exchanging greetings, Luciano tried to explain to himself why his friend's question had that tone to it. He couldn't help but observe his father's appearance more closely. The threadbare elbows of his shirt and the raveled stitch in his pants momentarily took on a moral significance in his eyes: he realized that Lima was no place to be poor, that here poverty was a dreadful stigma, obvious proof of a bad reputation.

"It's been a long time since I've seen him," he added without knowing why. "He's been on a trip."

"I've been in the south," the old man verified. "A good many business trips to Santiago, Buenos Aires . . . I have a business, wine along with hardware, but now, with the duty on imports and foreign currency, things are going . . ."

All of a sudden he stopped talking. The young man looked at him with astonishment. Luciano noticed his hands were beginning to perspire.

"Won't you all have a drink?" the old man added. "It'll be on me."

"We'll do it another time," Luciano impatiently intervened. "We have to finish our game. Where can I meet you?"

"Wherever you want. I've already told you I'm going to Callao."

"I'll walk you to the gate."

They both started for the exit in silence.

"You shouldn't have made me go in there," the old man stammered. "What will your friends say?"

"What are they going to say?"

"Well, elegant people come here. You have to dress fancy, in tailored pants, right?"

"If you'll come by the house, I can give you some shirts."

The old man looked at him angrily. "You're not going to dress me now; I'm the one who bought you your first pair of shoes!"

Luciano tried to remember what shoes his father had referred to. Suddenly, from the door facing an alleyway, he saw all his childhood memories rushing back to him in bare feet. Nevertheless, when they got to the fence, he took all the money he had from his pocket. "Santa Rosa Garden at six o'clock," he murmured as he put out his hand.

When the old man finished counting the money, he looked up but Luciano was already at a distance, as though wanting to spare his father an embarrassing display of gratitude.

Shortly after six, Luciano arrived at Santa Rosa Garden. In an attack of vanity, he had put on his best suit, his finest shoes, and a gold tie clasp, as if he hoped to show his father he couldn't care less about all the years he wasn't at home, that his absence had been, on the contrary, one of the reasons for his success.

This was not quite true, however, and nobody knew better than Luciano the humiliation his mother had endured so he could finish high school. Nobody knew better than he that the prosperity written all over his attire as well as his affiliation with the club—where he was on equal footing with the older members and got drunk with their sons—was a provisional, threatened prosperity, maintained by shady business deals. If the club tolerated him, it was certainly not because of social equality but because Luciano, aside from being a tireless "sparring partner," knew the members' weaknesses, and was the secret agent of their vices, linking the underworld to the drawing room.

The first thing he saw when he walked through the door was his father, under the grape arbor, drinking liquor and talking with two men. He stopped and observed him for a moment. His father looked like he had been sitting there for hours, maybe since they had left one another at the club. He had loosened his tie and was making exaggerated gestures with his hands. His companions were listening to him, amused. Customers at other tables were pricking up their ears in order to catch fragments of his chatter.

Luciano's arrival must have unsettled him because his hand, poised in mid air, was unable to finish outlining the gesture it had begun; it was like seeing an object taking shape before your very eyes, then suddenly evaporating into thin air. His father quickly got up and added to the show by knocking over a chair.

"He's here now!" he exclaimed, as he took a few steps forward with his arms extended. "What did I tell you? My *ñato* has arrived!"

Luciano saw him coming and regrettably found himself pressed against his father's chest. He endured his fierce embrace for what seemed to be an interminable length of time. A whiff of cheap liquor and the pungent smell of onion penetrated his nostrils. Suddenly moved by this gesture, his hands tightened around his father's shoulders and impulsively, held him close. After all these years, a good hug wasn't so bad.

"Let's go sit down," the old man said. "I'll introduce you to some friends here, all very nice boys. They're bank employees. I just met them."

Luciano took a seat and served himself a *pisco* to please his father. The employees were observing him with puzzlement. His tie clasp, and especially the ruby on his finger, seemed to leave them bewildered. They couldn't see any real connection between that greasy old chatterbox and the mestizo with the airs of a dandy.

"The boy's an engineer," the old man lied. "He studied at La Molina. He always made good grades. I did too, when I was in the College of . . . Do you remember, Luciano?"

Luciano was quiet and let his father talk. Coming to this meeting, his first intention was to pelt the old man with questions, cornering him and forcing him back to the years when he had abandoned him, giving himself a chance to unleash all his resentments. However, the employees' presence and his first *pisco* discouraged him from doing it. He began to forget about his clothing, his animosity, and to penetrate the fictitious world men create when they sit around an open bottle. Gazing toward the back of the garden, he saw a group of customers playing *bochas*.[3] Now and then his father would ask him to verify some tale he was spinning and he would mechanically repeat: "It's true." The sound of his voice stirred those deadened zones of his memory. There was that soccer game his father took him to as a child, and those silver coins that gave him access to a paradise filled with *turrones*.[4]

"Let's play a game of *sapo*!"[5] the old man exclaimed. "Hey, you, good sir, give me the bad news!"

The waiter came up. Luciano saw himself being led over to a corner by his father.

"Eh, do you have some extra coins? These two bankers are drinking me dry. You just wait! We'll make up for it with this game."

Luciano settled up with the waiter while his father made his way over to the game area with the employees. He was talking in a loud voice as he went, slapping the waiters on the back, making jokes with the other customers, and butting in on all the arguments. He had the ambivalent look of a peddler and a carnival recruiter and the husky voice of a boozer which quickly made him popular; at times he seemed like the oldest veteran customer of the place.

"Where's the manager?" he shouted. "Tell him that Don Francisco, president of the Huarasino Club, is here to offer him the club special!"

Luciano hurried over to him. He felt the need to be at his side, ostensibly to reveal his ties to that man who dominated the garden playground. Taking him quickly by the arm, he walked beside him.

3. Bowling.
4. Candies made with almond paste.
5. *Sapo* is Spanish for frog. In Peru it is a popular game in which players throw chips at a large, metal replica of a frog that contains several holes or openings of varying numerical value, with the frog's mouth highest in value. The player who earns the most points wins the game.

The old man confided in a whisper: "I've bet the employees a dozen bottles of Cristal."

"But I don't know how to play!"

"Leave that up to me!"

The chips began to fly toward the frog's mouth. The employees, who were a little drunk, threw them like stones, skinning the paint off the back wall. His father, on the other hand, measured his shots and executed his throws with impeccable style. Luciano never grew tired of observing him; he believed he had discovered in him a kind of hidden refinement, something that a miserable, vulgar life had smothered but not completely destroyed. He wondered how his father would look in a smart vest and told himself how good it would be to give him the most expensive one he could find.

Meanwhile, the bottles of Cristal were being guzzled up. The old man seemed rejuvenated with each swig, assuming legendary stature. His unbridled euphoria was contagious, and Luciano told himself they had the whole evening ahead of them and they had to make good use of it. The employees became obstacles. One of them fell down vomiting under the arbor, and the other tried to pick him up.

"Let's go! They're as good as dead!"

"Not yet!" the old man protested, so Luciano had to follow him through all the side cubicles, join in his conversations, and finally watch him as he played a game of *bochas* in his shirtsleeves, thundering like a titan, annihilating his adversaries.

"That's how the *porteños*[6] play!" he shouted, while the small pins flew through the air.

Luciano finally succeeded in convincing him they should leave.

"More carousing?" the old man inquired.

"We'll go to Once Amigos de Bolognesi in the Victoria district where my real buddies are!"

They left Santa Rosa Garden, embracing each other and singing as they took out through the streets of Magdalena looking for a taxi.

At the club, a vacant garage which they entered through a back door, there were a dozen questionable-looking characters playing *craft*,[7] checkers, smoking, and drinking beer. The uproar Luciano created as he went in caused everyone to turn around and look.

6. Inhabitants of a port city, in this case, Callao, Peru.
7. The men are shooting craps.

"Señores!" he shouted when he got to the center of the room. "I'd like you to meet my father!"

Everybody got quiet as they watched the strange, fat man who leaned against the counter to keep from falling over, his tie loosened, and the remainder of his hair haphazardly twisted around the bald spot on the back of his head. Luciano started toward the tables, toppling the game boards and dice boxes as he went.

"The game's over! Now everybody drinks with us. A father like this one doesn't come along every day. We ran into each other on the street. I haven't seen him for eight years."

Some of the guys protested, others tried to resume their game, arguing over the position of the chips, but when they heard Luciano send the bartender for some bottles of champagne, they resigned themselves to honoring the newcomer.

"He even has your same jaw!" one said, going up to the old man to shake his hand. Others got up and embraced him. The first toasts were made.

"Behind locked doors!" Luciano said, shutting the back door. "Not even the cops can get in here."

The tables were pushed together to create a huge surface. The first drink pulled the old man out of his stupor and, after letting loose some cuss words in order to clear his throat, he prepared to make himself worthy of their attention. Beginning with remarks, then anecdotes, he gradually controlled all the conversation. When the bartender arrived with the champagne, he was the only one talking. His stories, mostly invented and told in savory Creole jargon, were sometimes broken off, taken up again, retold in a different way, spiced with crude sayings of his own invention, along with references to popular waltzes; all provoked bursts of laughter.

Luciano silently witnessed the whole scene from a corner of the room. His eyes, instead of resting on his father, were scanning the faces of his friends. He read their delight and surprise as signs of paternal existence: his sense of abandonment was ending. That man with the big, beardless jaw whom he had hated and forgotten for so many years, now had become such an opulent reality that he considered himself a poor extension of him, a gift from his very being. How could he repay him? He could give him money, keep him in Lima, or make him a business partner. It didn't seem like enough. He got up mechanically and slowly, cautiously went up to him. When he was in front of him, he took him by the shoulders and forcefully kissed him on the mouth.

The old man, interrupted, ducked down in his chair. Everybody laughed. Luciano was perplexed. Opening his arms as though offering an apology, he returned to his seat. His father went on with his story after wiping his lips with his sleeve.

He was talking about women. Luciano suddenly felt sad. A bit of liquid remained at the bottom of his champagne glass. He poked its bubbles with a match stick while he remembered his mother whom he would visit now and then in the back alley, taking her fruit or handkerchiefs. He was losing his train of thought. Someone was talking about going to the red-light district of La Victoria. It was always like that in men's groups, no matter how large; the moment always came when everyone felt profoundly alone.

But that wasn't what bothered him. It was his father's voice. It was closing in on a dangerous zone, making mock attacks. Luciano felt tempted to bury his head in his hands and cover his ears. It was too late.

"And how's the old lady?"

The question came from the other end of the table, through all the bottles. It produced silence. Luciano looked at his father and tried to smile.

"She's fine," he answered and looked down into his empty glass again. "She hasn't missed you either. She's never asked about you."

"I haven't laid eyes on her in eight or ten years," the old man went on, addressing the group. "How time flies! We get old . . . isn't there any more champagne for me? . . . We used to live in a little back alley, we lived like pigs, isn't that right, Luciano? I couldn't stand it . . . a man like myself, well, without any freedom . . . always looking at the same face, smelling the same woman, shit, I had to get out and see the world and I left . . . Yes sir, I left!"

Luciano squeezed the glass, hoping it would shatter. It resisted.

"Besides . . ." the old man continued, smiling slyly. "I, I . . . she, if Luciano will pardon me, but the truth is she, you all understand, she . . ."

"Shut up!" Luciano shouted as he got to his feet.

" . . . she slept with everybody!"

The group exploded with laughter. In a flash Luciano found himself beside his father. When everyone stopped laughing, they noticed that the old man's lips were bloody. Luciano had him by his tie and his bobbing head kept hitting the big doughy face.

"Grab him, grab him!" the old man shouted.

It took four of them to grab him and drag him off to a corner. His small body was writhing, and he was panting with furor.

"If you want to fight, go out onto the street!" someone exclaimed. "You'll tear up the nice furniture in here!"

After a struggle in which everyone intervened—not being sure if they were to restrain them or kick them out—Luciano and his father found themselves on the street.

"To Humboldt Avenue," Luciano said, and resolutely took out walking while he straightened his tie and smoothed his hair. His father followed him with short, hurried steps.

"Wait! Why so far?"

When he caught up with him, he walked beside him, still drunk, talking in a loud voice, hurling insults at him.

"You mean you didn't know? With everybody! Who do you think paid for the food then?"

When they reached Humboldt Avenue, they began looking for a dark street. Luciano was feeling tired, thinking about hundreds of ways to face his corpulent, heavy rival: to avoid a hand-to-hand fight, bluff him with a sham attack until he could wear him out, or get dirt in his eyes, or sneak a stone into his coat pocket.

"Here," the old man said, pointing to a semidark street in the middle of which hung a yellow light. They left their coats on the fender of an abandoned taxi and rolled up their sleeves. Luciano tucked the cuffs of his pants in the top of his socks. Squaring off, they faced each other.

Luciano saw that his father's guard was down and his huge belly made an open target for him. Still, he took a few steps back. The old man drew closer. Luciano again backed away. The old man kept on advancing.

"Are you going to fight me? Watch out. I'll flatten you."

Luciano had backed against a wall, so he used his hands to spring forward. With one leap he regained the distance and now was ready to strike a blow with his fist when he noticed an expression, a simple expression of alarm or of fear on his father's face, forcing him to leave his fist suspended in the air. The old man was motionless. They both looked each other in the eye as though they were about to let out a cry. Luciano still had time to think—"It's as though I'm looking at myself in the mirror"—when he felt the heavy hand swing at his breastbone and the other one graze his nose. Regaining his balance, he stepped back and greeted the advancing form with a kick in the belly. The old man fell backward.

Luciano quickly stepped over him, picked up his jacket, and ran toward the corner. When he reached Humboldt Avenue, he abruptly stopped. The body was still there, looking like an animal that had been run over and abandoned in the middle of the road. He carefully went back to him. As he bent over, he saw that the old man was sleeping and snoring soundly. Taking him by his legs, he dragged him over to the sidewalk. Then, he leaned over him again to take one last look at his massive jaw, at that illusion of a father that he was seeing for the last time. Yanking his ring from his finger, he placed it on the vanquished man's little finger, with the ruby facing toward his palm. Lighting a cigarette, he pensively walked away toward the bars of La Victoria.

BERLIN, 1958

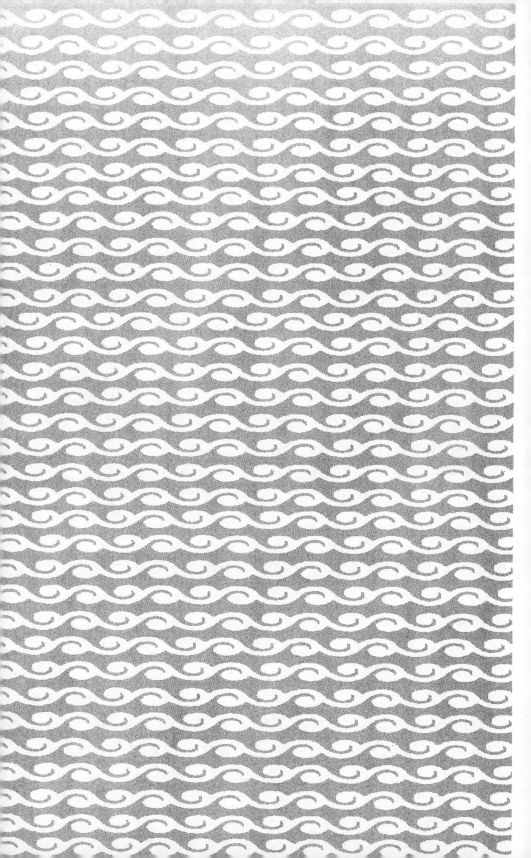

Nothing to Do, Monsieur Baruch

*M*onsieur Baruch remained totally impervious to the fact that the postman was still tossing advertisements under his door. Over the last three days the mailman had slipped him a pamphlet from the Society of Galvantherapy showing a guy with a cretin face on the front page under the heading "Thanks to Doctor Klein's method I am now a happy man"; there was also an ad for Ajax detergent that offered a five-cent discount on the family size if purchased within ten days; finally there were instructive brochures offering Sir Winston Churchill's memoirs payable in fourteen monthly installments, a complete home carpentry kit whose principal feature was an electric drill, and an especially colorful flyer about the art of writing and editing, which the postman tossed with such skill that it just about flew straight into Monsieur Baruch's hand. But inspite of the fact that Monsieur Baruch was very close to the door with his eyes fixed upon it, he couldn't care less about these things; he had been dead for three days.

Exactly three days ago today Monsieur Baruch awakened in the middle of the afternoon, after a completely sleepless night during which he tried to remember in order all the beds he had slept in during the last twenty years and all the songs that were popular in his youth. The first thing he did when he got up was to start for the kitchen sink to see if it was still clogged up, and if he would have to fill the pan with water in order to wash up, dipping only his fingers and the tip of his nose in it, like he had been doing for the past few days.

Then, without bothering to take his pyjamas off, he tackled a problem that had plagued him since Simón let him have the house a year ago, a problem he had never been able to solve: which of the two rooms of this apartment should be the combination living-dining room and which one the bedroom-study? Ever since arriving at the house, he had weighed the pros and cons of an eventual decision, but each day brought different objections that prevented him from actually taking any action. His indecisiveness stemmed from the fact that both rooms were absolutely symmetrical in relation to the front door, which overlooked a small vestibule only big enough for a coat rack. In addition, both rooms were similarly furnished: each had a sofa bed, a table, an armoire, two chairs, and a boarded-up fireplace. The difference rested in the fact that the room on the right opened onto the kitchen and the one on the left onto the bathroom. Making the room on the right into a bedroom would put the toilet out of immediate reach, a place he had to go with unusual frequency because of the recurring effect of a weak bladder; using the room on the left as the bedroom meant moving away from the kitchen and his nocturnal cups of coffee, which for him had become a necessity of almost a spiritual order.

For these reasons Monsieur Baruch, since he came to live in that house, had alternately slept in one room or the other and eaten at one table or the other, according to the successive and always provisional solutions he kept finding for his dilemma. This kind of nomadism that he was practicing in his own house had produced in him a paradoxical sensation: on the one hand, it gave him the impression of living in a bigger house because he could say that he had two living-dining rooms and two bedroom-studies; at the same time, he realized that in reality the rooms' similarities made his house smaller, since it was a matter of a useless duplication of space, like that effected by a mirror; he couldn't find anything in the second room that the first one didn't have, and to combine them was deceptive, like when someone taking inventory of the titles in his library tries to count two exact copies of the same book.

Monsieur Baruch couldn't solve the problem that day either, so he left it pending one more time and returned to the kitchen to prepare breakfast. With his steaming cup of coffee in one hand and dry toast in the other, he sat down at the nearest table, meticulously took note of his frugal meal, then moved to the table in the adjacent room where a folder with writing paper awaited him. He picked up a sheet, wrote some brief lines on it, and put it in an envelope. On the envelope he wrote: Madame Renée Baruch, 17 Rue de la Joie, Lyon. And below that, with a red ink pen, he added: personal and urgent.

Leaving the envelope conspicuously on the table, Monsieur Baruch mentally plotted the rest of his daily tasks, focusing on two things he habitually did before facing the night one more time: buy a newspaper and prepare another cup of coffee and dry toast. While he was waiting for nightfall, he wandered from one room to the other, peering through their respective windows. The one on the right overlooked the corridor of a factory—he never found out what it made—but which most likely was a place of penance, since only black, Algerian and Iberian workers came there. The one on the left overlooked part of a street where cars were continuously going by with their headlights already turned on. A fire truck also passed by, blowing its siren. A house was burning in the distance.

Monsieur Baruch prolonged his stroll longer than usual, already convincing himself that he shouldn't buy the newspaper. With the exception of the work ads, he never finished reading the paper nor did he understand what they were saying: What did the Vietnamese want? Who was Señor Lacerda? What was an electronic computer? Where was Karachi located? As he wandered about this time at dusk, he again heard a little sound inside his head; it was not coming, he discovered, from Madame Pichot's television, or from Señor Belmonte's water heater, or from the typewriter Señor Ribeyro was writing on above him. It was a noise like a train car makes disengaging from the stopped engine and setting off unexpectedly on a trip of its own.

Full of doubt, he paused for a moment in the dark apartment beside the light switch. What if he went out for a walk? He hardly knew the neighborhood. Ever since he arrived he had studied the shortest route to the bakery, the metro, and the market, and he had fastidiously stuck to it. One time he dared to deviate from his route, only to end up in a horrible, circular area called the Plaza de la Reunión, with its dirt surface, dusty trees, cracked benches, stray dogs, crippled old men, groups of Algerians without jobs or houses, good God, filthy houses, joyless and merciless, looking at each other with terrified faces, as if any minute they would let out a cry and disappear in an explosion of shame.

Abandoning all thoughts of a walk, Monsieur Baruch turned on the light in the room where he had left the letter, making sure it was still there, crossed the next room in the dark, and went into the kitchen. He carefully shaved himself in five minutes, put on a clean suit, and returned to the lavatory mirror to look at his face. There was nothing different or unusual about it. His prolonged regimen of coffee and toast had sunken his cheeks, true; his nose, which he always viewed with certain commiseration because of its tendency to bow over the years, was now suspended between his cheeks like a droopy flag signaling defeat. His eyes, however, still had their usual expression of terror caused by traffic, drafts of air, movies, beautiful women, asylums, hoofed animals, and those lonely nights that caused him to start and cover his heart when some stranger stopped him on the street to ask him the time of day.

It had to be time for the afternoon movie because a virile voice was coming from his neighbor's television, a voice that could very well belong to Jean Gabin playing a police commissioner as he spoke in slang with a cigarette between his lips; but Monsieur Baruch, indifferent to the emotion that undoubtedly was engulfing Madame Pichot, limited himself to rinsing out his razor, removing the blade, and turning off the light. He stepped fully dressed into the shower which was inside a little metallic cubicle in a corner of the kitchen, turned on the faucet and let the cold water gradually wet his head, neck, and suit. Tightly grasping the razor blade between his forefinger and the thumb on his right hand, he raised his jaw and made a short, but deep incision on his throat. The pain he felt was less intense than he had expected, tempting him to repeat the process again. He finally decided to sit down in the shower with his legs crossed and began to wait. His clothes were soaked by now, making him shiver and raise his arm to shut off the faucet. When the last drops stopped falling on his head, he experienced a warm, almost peaceful sensation in his chest, reminding him of the sunny mornings in Marseilles, when he would go to the bars of the port offering, without much luck, ties to the sailors, and also of those other Genoese mornings when he would help out Simón with his dry goods store. Then he recalled the trips he had planned to Lithuania, where, they told him, he was born, and to Israel, where he must have had close relatives whom he imagined to be numerous, and onto whose faces he sketched his own.

Yet another fire truck passed in the distance, blowing its siren and he told himself that it was absurd to be closed up in that dark, wet cubicle like someone atoning for a sin or hiding from a bad act (but hadn't his entire life been a bad act?) and how much better it was to stretch out on the sofa in one of the rooms and by doing that, create a new room in the house, the mortuary chamber, a room he always knew potentially existed and that had been luring him ever since he arrived.

He didn't have any difficulty standing up and leaving the shower. But when he was about to abandon the kitchen, he felt a retching that left him doubled over, vomiting so violently that he lost his balance. Before he could lean against the wall, he found himself lying on the floor under the lintel, with his legs in the kitchen and his trunk in the adjoining room. The light was still on in the next room and from his facedown position Monsieur Baruch could see the table, and along the table's edge, the cover of the folder with writing paper.

He mentally explored his body, searching for some sign of pain, some fracture, some serious damage that would indicate that his mortal machine was definitively nonfunctional. Yet he wasn't feeling any discomfort. He knew only that it was impossible to stand and if he had learned anything else, it was that from now on he should forget about living a vertical life and be contented with the sluggish existence of an earthworm and its relentless, inane chores, flush with the ground, suffering in the dust from which it emerged.

Then he began a long trip over the floor strewn with flyers and old newspapers. His arms were heavy, so he tried to inch forward using his jaw and his shoulders, bending his waist and scraping the floor with the tips of his shoes. He paused for awhile trying to remember where he had left that long bandage he wrapped around his waist every winter to combat his sciatica. If he had left it in the armoire in the first room, he would only have to move about thirteen feet to reach it. Otherwise, the trip would be about as unlikely as him returning to Lithuania or making a round trip to the kingdom of Zion.

While Monsieur Baruch reminisced, debating whether the draft of air on him was getting a little sharper and harder to breathe, and while he recalled everything he had done for the past few weeks and mentally imagined the objects stored in all the drawers in the house, he heard the firemen's siren; this time it was accompanied by the sound of a creaking train car as it disengages and picks up speed, rushing through the flat countryside, with neither an itinerary nor destination, passing but not seeing the rural stations, the beautiful spots marked with a cross on the tourist brochures, indifferent, intoxicated, unaware of anything but its own speed and shabby state, isolated, only destined to end up lost on an abandoned route where nothing but decay and oblivion awaited him.

Maybe his eyelids shut or an opaque substance filled his exposed eyeballs because he stopped seeing his house, armoires, and tables and saw, yes, clearly this time, unexpectedly, by the light of an interior projector, miraculously, the beds he had slept in over the past twenty years, including the last double bed in Marais' store, where Renée would roll into a ball on her side, forbidding him to cross some ideal, geometrical line running down the middle of the bed. There were the beds in hotels, boarding houses, shelters, always narrow, impersonal, rough, unpleasant, one rigorously following another in time with not a single one missing and filling space with a nocturnal, hellish train over which he crawled like he was doing now, spending endless nights, alone, seeking refuge from his terror. What he couldn't make out, though, were the songs, except for dissonant croaking sounds, as if dozens of radio stations were interfering, struggling to outdo each other, only succeeding in emitting disjointed words, perhaps from popular song titles, like treason, infidelity, loneliness, any word, anguish, vengeance, summer, words with no tune falling harshly on his ears like dominos, or maybe suggesting a charade or giving a bare outline of a chapter of some mediocre, impassioned drama, not catastrophic like those printed in the crime section of the daily newspapers.

The tapping of the guitar's bass string ended abruptly and Monsieur Baruch realized that he could see again, he saw the inaccessible lamp in the adjoining room and under the lamp, the inaccessible folder with the letters. The silence in which familiar objects were now floating was worse than blindness. If only it would begin raining on the thin tin or if Madame Pichot would turn up the volume on her television set or if it would occur to Señor Belmonte to take a late night bath; any noise, no matter how slight or shrill, would rescue him from the world of the present, silent things that, when deprived of sound, seemed hollow, deceptive, as if cunningly distributed by some astute scenographer to make him believe he was still in the realm of the living.

But he didn't hear anything, nor did he have any luck remembering in which corner of the house he had left the bandage for his sciatica; the most he could do was to proceed with his trip, as hopeless as it was, since the newspapers were crumpled up ahead of him, creating a pile of undulating obstacles through which he felt incapable of clearing a path. Focusing his eyes, he read a headline in bold type, SHEILA ACCUSES, and below that, in more discrete print, Lord Chalfont asserts that the value of the pound sterling will not go down, and to the side of that a rectangular section announcing a typhoon sweeping the northern Philippines; finally, in almost invisible print requiring much tenacity on his part to decipher, he read "Monsieur and Madame Lescene are pleased to announce the birth of their grandson Luc-Emmanuel." Then he once again felt the warm sensation, the pleasant breeze in his chest, and instantly he heard Bernard's voice telling Renée that if they didn't give him a raise he would quit Marais' store and then Renée's voice saying that the boy deserved a raise and his own voice advising him to wait for awhile and the stairs creaking the first time he tiptoed down to spy as they talked and joked behind the counter, among pocketbooks, umbrellas, and gloves and a ripping sound that could only be the note Renée left before she ran out on him, written on notebook paper, and which he tore into bits and pieces after reading it several times, stupidly thinking that if he destroyed the evidence he would destroy the crime.

The voices and noises either faded or Monsieur Baruch refused to pick up on them because when he turned his eyes, he noted something that forced him suddenly to change all his plans: the door leading to the street was closer to him than the armoires of both rooms and the unlikely bandage. Through the lower slot he saw the light from the stairlanding. He then began to rotate on his stomach, with extreme difficulty, trying to change the initial direction of his itinerary while the light from the landing came on and went off several times and footsteps on what seemed to be a circular staircase or on the lower floors or in the basement because they never, never seemed to reach him.

After making an effort to change direction, his head was no longer supported by his jaw, but rather fell heavily to one side, resting on an ear.

The walls and roof were spinning now; the fireplace passed before his eyes several times, followed by the armoire, sofa, and other pieces of furniture; behind him a lamp and other objects were chasing one another in circles, more recklessly each time round. Monsieur Baruch held in reserve one last recourse until that moment; he tried to scream, but in all the chaos, who could guarantee where his mouth, tongue, and throat were? Everything was scattered about and his relationship to his body had become so vague that he really didn't know his own shape, length, or how many extremities he had. By now the whirlwind had stopped and what he saw at the moment, right before his eyes, was a piece of newspaper where he read "Monsieur and Madame Lescene are pleased to announce the birth of their grandson Luc-Emmanuel."

He abandoned his efforts and himself over the dusty papers. He hardly felt the presence of his body floating in watery space or immersed and at the bottom of a well. Now he was lithely swimming in a sea of vinegar. No, it wasn't a sea of vinegar, but a calm lake. A bird chirped in the foliage of a tree. Water was flowing through the rough, green brook. The moon was rising in a diaphanous sky. Cows were grazing in the fertile pasture. By some strange bend in the river he had come upon a pleasant landscape of the classics, where everything was music, order, lightness, reason, and harmony. Finally, everything made sense. Now he understood, without any argument, apodictically, he should have made the room where he left the bandage into the bedroom or left the bandage in the room where the bedroom was going to be and he should have thrown Bernard out of the store and turned Renée in for running off with the money and pursued her to Lyon begging her on his knees to come back and told Renée to leave without Bernard knowing about it and killed himself that very night she ran off so he wouldn't have suffered for a whole year and paid an assassin to stab Bernard or Renée or both of them or even himself on the steps of a synagogue and gone to Lithuania leaving Renée penniless and in his youth married the woman with only one breast who worked at the Marseilles boarding house and kept his money in the bank instead of in the house and made the room where he was lying into the bedroom and not gone out that first time when Renée asked him to the Café des Sports and set out on that merchant ship for Buenos Aires and let himself grow a thick mustache sometime and kept the bandage in the armoire nearby so that, now that he was dying far from his pleasant homeland and instead collapsed on top of filthy obstacles, he could have attempted an extreme cure, to give himself some time, to survive, tear up the suicide note, write it the next day or the next year, and still continue walking through the house, in his sixties, tired, with no job, talent, or skill, no Renée and no income, watching the mysterious factory or the roof of the garage or listening to how the water ran down through the pipes from upstairs or to Madame Pichot turning on her television set.

Finally, everything was possible. Monsieur Baruch stood up, but in reality he was still lying down. He cried out, but only had a grimace on his face. He lifted an arm, but only managed to open his hand. That's why after three days, when the police knocked down the door, we found him stretched out, looking at us; if it hadn't been for the flies and the black puddle, we would have thought he was acting out a pantomime, waiting for us there on the floor with his arm outstretched, anticipating our greetings.

PARIS, 1967

The Captives

~~~~~~~

*I*t was the last thing I expected: to live in that bourgeois boarding house on the outskirts of Frankfurt, in an industrial district surrounded by chimneys, trams, and busy, efficient early risers, exposing my slothful, useless nature with their hustle and bustle. It was a boarding house for transients, Hanseatic salesmen, circumspect propagandists selling some obscure product, none of whom ever appeared in the corridors wearing pajamas; they were incapable of taking an interest in that exotic boarder who wandered about, slipping over the immaculate linoleum, unsure of himself, thinking absurd thoughts, profoundly sad, like a camel lost on the polar continent.

The truth is, I wasn't idle. A romantic friend of mine who was forced into business had given me an assignment, promising to pay my travel expenses, to find out about the latest procedures for four-color printing, a subject I couldn't care less about. But since my friend was on the other side of the Atlantic, I performed his assignment in a very subjective way, content with snooping around some establishment from time to time, asking for technical explanations in German, which I listened to stoically. I combined my work with long walks through the city.

Downtown Frankfurt attracted me at first, but I ended up disliking it. In the majority of its streets, stores, and corner bars I would run into North American soldiers whom I recognized even when they weren't in uniform because of their closely cropped hair and wide pants, their strange slipperlike shoes, their mania for going around in groups, the little bracelets on their wrists, their clumsy gait, and the arrogant, cybernetic way they looked and gave orders.

That's why I chose my district for the forays, but its factories intimidated me. To me, nothing is more dreadful than a factory. I fear them because they fill me with ignorance and unanswerable questions. Sometimes when I'm observing them I ask myself why they've been constructed one way and not another, why there's a chimney here, a crane there, a drawbridge, a rail, an agglomerate of piping, pulleys, levers, and moving implements. It's clear that all those well-designed, programmed mechanical devices have been built for operating something indispensable. But at the same time, in order to build those devices, it's been necessary no doubt to build others before them, since nothing comes from nothing. Every machine, no matter how simple, requires an earlier one to produce it. In this guise, for me a factory is the result of an infinite number of former factories, every tool coming from a preceding tool perhaps increasingly smaller and simpler, but whose link dates from the beginning of the industrial age, or even further back to the Renaissance, or even further yet, to prehistoric times, so at the end of our quest we find only one tool, neither created nor invented, but perfect: the hand of man.

However, finding the human hand as the origin of the industrial miracle satisfied my intelligence, but it didn't appease my boredom or my fatigue. In reality, Frankfurt was an overly organized metropolis, too capitalistic and powerful for my ancestral, Catonian fondness for nature.

Nevertheless, nature was present at the Hartman boarding house and one morning I discovered it. I woke up very early that day and decided to take a bath. In order to do so, I had to cross the entire boarding house on the way to the bathroom. It was located at the rear of the building that bordered on, I supposed, one of those dreary patios that is every traveler's terror, where rugs were shaken or where some bush languished in a flowerpot. When I opened the upper window halfway in order to prevent the hot water from steaming over the mirrors, I discovered nature itself. It came to me like an extremely vibrant, subtle instrumental concerto. Could the chirping be coming from a distant forest? Could it be a pleasant reminder of home coming to me through song, through a swelling of musical vibrations? Was it the song of all the birds of paradise?

Climbing over the tub, I peeked through the window and saw a radiant spectacle: in the early morning hundreds of birds in huge wire cages were jumping around and chirping. The Hartman boarding house had an enormous garden filled with bird cages. The large cages were arranged along both sides of a passageway through which a corpulent, gray-haired man in a robe with a basket under his arm, was going around distributing food to the birds. I observed the loving way he was talking to them, caressing them with his finger through the wires, and feeding them. It was truly an extraordinary, unreal sight, like seeing a line from an eclogue quoted in the annual budget of an insurance firm.

As soon as I finished bathing, I dressed and went down to the first floor to look for the enchanted garden. I had to walk down a long corridor, go through several doors, cross the large kitchen, the office, and the storeroom in order to reach an interior terrace leading to the place with the songbirds.

The man in the robe saw me and kept standing in the middle of the passageway, the basket in his hand, observing me. The birds abruptly stopped singing.

"What are you doing here?"

"I'm a boarder."

The man angrily approached me and stopped barely inches away from my nose, which he examined like an anatomist, then my ears and the shape of my skull with a wariness that seemed slowly to dissipate.

"You're not German?"

"I'm South American."

The man observed my features again and his surliness vanished.

"All right. I'm Mr. Hartman, and I own the boarding house. I'll let you in here because you're a foreigner. Are you interested in birds?"

"I heard them singing when I was in the bathroom. I took the liberty of coming down here."

"You can watch them if you like."

The first cage that I went to was for canaries. There were at least a hundred with silkaline plumage that went from blue-gray to the most brilliant yellow. As soon as they saw Hartman they began to jump on their swings and chirp, eliciting echoes from other cages, the beginning of a concerto that soon reached an irresistible crescendo. Hartman intervened with a strange, penetrating modulated sound, half whistle, half cry, and the concerto ceased at once.

"They know me. They're very disciplined. Do you want to see the exotic birds?"

The passage was intersected by another corridor, also covered with bird cages. In one of them I saw a moving palette of reds and greens. It was the cage with parrots. Hartman named them for me, showed me the difference between parrots, parakeets, magpies, and red-and-blue macaws, explained the origin and peculiarities of each with an exactness and knowledge that astonished me.

"Are you an ornithologist?" I asked, finally.

The owner smiled and with a wide sweep of his arm tossed a little canary seed at the cage.

"Just an amateur. I've always liked birds grouped together like this in their cages. They're so obedient, so submissive, and, when you think about it, quite defenseless. Their life depends totally on me."

From that day on, before beginning my laborious visits to the printing offices to gather data for my friend, I went down to the garden two or three times a week to keep Hartman company as he made his morning rounds. Since winter was coming, he was preparing the cages to withstand the cold and the snow. There was a folded canvas tarpaulin on top of each that he had started to spread out.

"Some species are very fragile, especially those from countries with hot climates. The first cold snap breaks them like a piece of straw."

I realized some of the cages even had a heating system similar to hot water radiators.

"Your birds certainly do live like princes."

"Do you think so? Perhaps, but like captive princes."

When I asked him about a white, wading bird with black wings and a long beak for poking at the ground, he said to me, "He's one of my treasures. An ibis who comes from Egypt; he likes earthworms."

"I know. They talk about him in the *Book of the Dead*. I believe there are even sketches of this bird on Egyptian pottery."

"Well, I see you know a thing or two. If you're interested I'll show you my books one of these afternoons."

In fact, one of those afternoons he came to my room. It was the hour when the boarders would gather in the living room to watch television and drink beer while waiting for supper to be served. Hartman came with a book under his arm. Sitting down on the edge of my bed, he opened it and invited me to look at the photographs with him. It was a book about hummingbirds. He was still explaining the variety of species to me when the maid knocked at the door for us to come down to the dining room.

"I'll show you another tomorrow," he said.

Then he started coming daily. A strong bond developed between us that had more to do with pedagogy than with friendship. Maybe Hartman discovered certain receptive qualities in me or saw me as the providential depository of his science and passion for birds. Each day he would bring a different book and initiate me in the mysteries of ornithology. Besides his erudition—he knew the anatomy, customs, and whims of each species—what I admired was his fervor. For him, talking about birds was like praying. I felt somewhat akin to the medieval disciple receiving from the master the keys to the arcanum via oral tradition.

After several days, when, I suppose, he thought my initiation over, he came to see me without any books and told me that I could visit his library. He took me there himself. It was on the third floor, at the back of the building, and was undoubtedly the biggest room in the boarding house. Two or three thousand books filled the shelves; there were bird illustrations on the walls, and on a mantel an entire collection of stuffed birds.

"I spend my life going from the garden to the library. No one is allowed in here. But you can come in when you want to look something up in a book. Of course, they're all on the same subject."

I thanked him for the invitation, and to show my gratitude, I asked him for a clue as to how to find my way around this labyrinth.

"I have a filing cabinet."

He pointed to a metal object.

As he led me to the file he started talking. "I know you're from South America, but I've never asked you which country you're from. There are so many."

"From Peru."

"Peru? A strange country. I don't know anything about it. I'm not very interested in history. I'll have to look it up in my encyclopedia. I do know about its birds—the *chaucato*,[1] for example, and the *huanchaco*[2]—and the *tuya* that sings high in the trees."

While I was distractedly looking through the card index, Hartman took a thick volume from a cabinet and pensively began to leaf through its pages.

"Peru, the Incas, Pizarro, viceroys. They don't talk much about your country here, or I should say they only talk about the past. I'm interested in more recent things. What can you tell me?"

"Whatever you want to know."

Hartman observed me carefully. An icy look. I felt like a bird in a cage.

"I'd rather look it up."

Then he told me I could choose a book and take it to my room, since he had to finish an article for a journal.

I selected a book on larks and left.

The next morning I received a letter from my friend and benefactor in Lima, urging me to depart quickly for Berlin. Since I had hardly worked on his assignments in Frankfurt—and did a poor job at that—I decided to make amends by spending those last days involved in incredibly boring research, forgetting about Hartman and his birds.

The evening prior to my departure, before going to buy my train ticket, I went down to the garden to take a last look at the birds and to tell Hartman good-bye. He was standing, dressed in a hat and coat, in the middle of the passage in front of the canaries' cage. When he saw me, instead of coming toward me with his hand extended like he always had

1. (Zool: *Mimus longi caudatus*). In Ica, Peru, *chaucato* is the name given to a small bird also called *corregidor*, *chauco*, and *choqueco*.

2. (Zool: *Pezites militaris bellicosa*). A small bird, very abundant in the flat, coastal plains and low, Andean slopes.

done, he turned around and kept his back toward me. I hesitated for a moment. His behavior seemed disturbing.

"Señor Hartman, I've come to say good-bye. I'm leaving for Berlin tomorrow at dawn."

"Kindly leave."

His order was so imperative that I was starting to go, when I saw him turn his head. His face was red, maybe because of the cold morning air.

"So you're from Peru, right? Wasn't it the first country in South America to declare war on Germany?"

I had forgotten that fact. Not only was it past history, but I thought it was insensitive of him to bring it up. He again turned his back on me, so I left.

In the evening, after packing my suitcases, I saw the book on larks that he had lent me. I hadn't even had time to look it over; it had been abandoned there on my night table from the first day. Picking it up, I headed for the library. I knocked on the door and, when no one answered, I opened it. No one was there. Hartman most likely had gone down to the kitchen for supper. Walking over to his desk, I placed the book on top of it. Then I saw on the blotting paper a *History of the Second World War* with a corner of a piece of hard, glossy paper sticking out of its closed pages. Out of curiosity I opened the book and a photograph of a strong, smiling officer in uniform slipped out; he was armed with a rifle, standing guard in front of a wire fence that could very easily be equated to a gigantic bird cage. Turning the photo over to look at the other side, I read: Hans Hartman, 1942, Auschwitz.

The piercing song of a thrush was coming from the garden. Looking out the window as night fell, I saw the jailor bending over a cage, lovingly conversing with one of his captives.

PARIS, 1971

The Spanish

I have lived in rooms both big and small, luxurious and wretched, but if there's one thing I've always looked for in a room, something more important than a good bed or a comfortable chair, it was a window overlooking the street. The most sordid space seemed tolerable if it had a window with a view of the street. The window very often compensated for an absent friend, a former girlfriend, or a book traded for a plate of beans. Through the window, I saw into the hearts of men and could comprehend the tales of the city.

Nevertheless, I was so poor that summer in Spain, I accepted a room without a view of the street; instead, it overlooked a neighboring patio. I've always detested these patios because looking at them is like seeing a building in its underwear. These patios are cold, gloomy boxes in winter, hot and noisy in summer, pierced by louvers, peepholes, and windows within windows behind which men come and go in suspenders, or old women cook; they have clothes hanging from lines, ledges used as pantries or flower stands, and lots of cats in the background who get skittish when we spit in their direction. There's no mystery to these patios because everything is much too evident; one only has to take a quick glance at them to behold all the nudity of the Madrileño colony.

That's why I spent several days, depressed, in this room with no bolt on the door—it was barred with a chair—looking at a trash can every morning, looking at a washbowl I emptied sleepy water in, and at the wardrobe with its cracked mirror, where I kept the only suit I hadn't hocked. Sometimes I would read or try to write. In the evenings I would go looking for some friend to play chess or for someone I could talk into inviting me for a bite to eat, with a glass of wine to go along with it. I didn't have any contact with the other boarders in the house, nor did I want any, fearing they would take pity on me; oh, they dined so well at the long table. I only saw the landlady regularly to tell her, with great sincerity, that I was waiting for a letter with money in it and that, meanwhile, could she advance me some *duros*[1]—green *duros* that quickly went up in smoke once they were in the hands of this hardened smoker.

That's how the summer went until finally, overcome by boredom, I decided to lean out the window to look at the neighboring patio. I would

---

1. A *duro* is a five-peseta piece.

do it in the evenings, when the breezes from the Guadarrama Mountains swept down and cooled things off. I would look with some sadness at all the windows, observing how first here, then there, a light went out or a song faded, leaving everything dark and silent except the deep blue sky, where stars were scattered about.

I don't know when it happened, but I'm sure it was one evening when I was absorbed in my thoughts, that I realized I wasn't alone: someone else was peering through the window on the right. Only the top half of a convulsive profile was visible, becoming alarmed as I stared harder. It was a young woman, and she disappeared when she saw me, closing the shutters behind her.

After several days I saw her again. My presence seemed to make her uneasy because every time she saw me, she either closed the window or stepped back, leaving a pair of pensive hands on the window ledge. I looked at those hands with passion, telling myself that anyone with a well-trained eye could read a person's entire history in the little finger. Examining it, however, I only came to the conclusion that this was a slender, graceful, spiritual, but unfortunate person.

Those hands intrigued me so much that I, a spider of sorts, busily weaving my vain table linen on paper, took the risk of walking the halls of the boarding house during the day. I ran into three cocottes, a silly old man in his pajama top, a student priest, a military man, and, worst of all, the landlady of the *duros*. However, I didn't see a trace of the girl with the convulsive profile.

Soon, though, a social event of utmost importance allowed me to meet her. It was the landlady's birthday. I noticed a lot of fuss in the house early that morning, and shortly before noon, Doña Candelas herself came to my room. "You're invited for dinner. Today's my birthday."

Later, when I went to the dining room with my gift—a bottle of Márquez del Riscal bought on credit in the store downstairs—all the boarders were gathered together. I recognized my neighbor right away; she was wearing a faded mustard-colored dress and, except for her light blue eyes, she had a pale look to her that only chastity, poverty, and Spanish boarding houses can bestow.

The tension diminished after the first dry sherries. The young priest was saying to one of the cocottes: "If you want to win over the opposition, you have to have good connections." The cocotte was saying to the old man in the pajama top: "I wash my face and hair with lemon every morning." The old man in the pajama top was saying to the military man: "No doubt the generalíssimo is a fortunate man." The military man was saying to Doña Candelas: "In Pasapoga, service costs forty pesetas."

Doña Candelas was saying to the student priest: "I'd rather have shrimp than gabardine."

The conversation went around the table, but there were two missing links in the long chain: Angustias and me. We looked at each other from afar and hardly opened our mouths. Not until the paella was served was I invited to tell something about my country, "the Indies," as the military man kept calling it. So I made three or four loony comments that amused the listeners. When I talked about the chili peppers, the old man in the pajama top smugly interrupted me: "We already know about it; your chili pepper is nothing but a red-hot pimiento."

That was all. In the evening, however, when I peered out the window, Angustias was there wearing her mustard-colored dress, and this time she didn't hide. We looked at the sky together and began a vague conversation about the constellations. Then she talked to me about Salamanca, its golden plaza and Roman cathedral, about the River Tormes, where frogs croak at dusk and students serenade in black capes with their guitars. When I went to bed, I held some threads of her destiny in my hands: I found out the old man in the pajama top was her father, they both lived in the same room, she almost never went out for anything, and I knew that what I read in her little finger was probably true; she was graceful, slender, spiritual, but unfortunate.

From then on I saw her fairly frequently, always at the window, at dusk. She lost some of her shyness each time and ended up telling me the story of her poverty. As I listened to her, I was asking myself how it was possible that this Salamancan flower, who in any other country would have incited greed and disputes, had to waste her twenty years of white breasts and white and brown belly in a dirty boarding house in Lavapies. I felt at a loss to do anything for her because, besides smoking on credit and accepting free food, I knew that Angustias, because of her extreme fragility, didn't turn me on but rather inspired in me a sort of protective passion. Besides, Dolli, the youngest of the cocottes, had exchanged some dewy-eyed looks with me, which promised an uncomplicated, prosaic adventure. During several of my sleepless nights, I saw her come in from the street and sadly hang on the patio clothesline her laundered panties, the trophy of so many battles.

Nevertheless, during that fleeting summer, I continued talking with Angustias, telling her about Madrid, its splendor, but also about the Caves of Ventosa, for example, where people had to burrow like moles in order to get inside them. I wanted to distract her, at least free her imagination which was always tightly bound to thimbles, pans, and four barren walls. I wanted to make a spectacle of myself for her. That's just it! I really was nothing but a spectacle in her eyes!

Finally Angustias fell in love, not with me of course, but with a young man who would court her when she went shopping at the fish market. She spoke to me about him several times, about his courtship and invitations. I accepted these intimate disclosures with a tinge of masculine jealousy typical of all men, but later I realized that Angustias' well-being depended on this providential love. I discreetly spied on the fellow and happily discovered he was one of those sincere Spaniards, a little obstinate, but sure of himself, and capable of performing any feat to win and protect his woman. A strong, one-woman man who, for lack of an imagination, envisioned marrying her. I encouraged Angustias to follow her heart, and because of my encouragement there was an autumn excursion at the Parque del Retiro complete with a boat ride and drizzle, and two or three movies where her pensive hands met for the first time those of the enamored brute. Soon after the romance began, however, a parenthesis of sudden fortune opened up for me, and I abandoned my window and its tales for awhile.

One morning I received the long-awaited money order. One must experience the most humbling limits of deprivation in order to truly know what it means suddenly to get your hands on fifteen thousand pesetas; prudence and providence become worthless. The first thing I did was have four suits custom-made in José Antonio's best shop. I then stocked up on light tobacco and good sherry. After that, I stripped a bookstore of its books, eagerly trying to catch up on my reading. Finally, after paying off my outstanding debts, I had some money left with which my virility laid claim to its most legitimate rights.

It was impossible to carry on an affair with the cocotte Dolli inside the boarding house; Spanish custom saw to that, only allowing me, within those confines, to converse with her about chaste subjects in which the student priest, the military man, or the landlady could take part. It was just a matter of going downstairs to the bar and phoning her in order to make a date.

We met on the Avenida de la Castellana, at one of those little outdoor tables that was still absorbing the warm days of autumn. We drank a delicious sherry and went dancing at Casablanca. It was an enchanting evening that ended as it should: in a room on San Marcos Street. After a week of going out together, I didn't have any money left. When Dolli realized she was paying for breakfast too often, she told me quite frankly: "Stud, I think we should end it. I have to make a living, you know."

She was right. I didn't have any choice but to shut myself up in my room, smoke cigarette butts, the cigarette butts of my memories, write, dream, and when I got bored, look out the window.

Angustias was there. I was hoping to encounter a happy face, but only saw a mask of misfortune. Her profile, more convulsive than ever, disdainfully spoke to me of life's vain pleasures, interwoven with infinite variations on the theme of resignation. She was telling me all this, of course, while playing with the threads dangling from the worn sleeves of her mustard-colored dress.

Later I found out that she had quarreled with her suitor over an invitation to go dancing at the Parrilla del Rex. According to the custom and practices of the Madrileños, dancing at the Parrilla del Rex was the solemn consecration of a dubious courtship. A romance can't prosper without observing this rite. He had invited her three times, and three times she had turned him down. The fourth time, he insisted they go dancing the next Saturday, threatening to break up with her if she didn't keep the date.

"I'm not going because I don't know how to dance," Angustias informed me.

Her excuse didn't seem reason enough, and it wasn't; later, she herself confessed to me that she wasn't going because she didn't have a dress to wear. It's hard to imagine how much a dress sometimes means in a woman's life. That afternoon, while strolling down the Gran Vía, I observed women in their dresses, and I realized how each one embodied the soul of her dress. I knew that often a woman's destiny depends on the price of a piece of cloth, and that it's possible to walk into a store and buy joy by the yards and happiness in a cardboard box.

As expected, Saturday came and I saw how Angustias, wearing her mustard-colored dress, was rapidly growing pale. Nothing I could say would console her. I began to see her father as an old fool in his pajama top, saying "providential generalíssimo" and drifting about Madrid selling pencils and ashtrays. I was tempted to shake him and say, "Buy your daughter a dress." But the poor fellow was smoking those dreadful Caldo de Gallina cigarettes and knew no other pleasure than that of his weekly game of dominos, which he played with other equally respectable old fools of the impoverished sector of Spanish society.

That Saturday I found myself just as distraught as Angustias. In an attempt to distract myself, I went to Dolli's room to enjoy her chitchat for awhile. Since our affair, I would frequently visit that big, fragrant room which the three cocottes shared. Dolli and Encarnita, who weren't overly pretentious, slept in the tidy twin beds like two nuns. Paloma, on the other hand, who only earned her pesetas in the elegant cabarets, had created in a corner of the room, with the help of a folding screen, a separate world complete with curtains, mirrors, and other signs of a rather questionable opulence. Since they didn't get up until one o'clock in the afternoon, it was easy to find them there in the mornings, lax and pallid after their latest obliging love affairs. I stretched out on the foot of Dolli's bed and, looking at the flat ceiling, talked with her and the others. When Paloma was in a good mood, she would get up singing, send me to buy some beer, and then, getting tipsy on it, would recite verses from García Lorca's poems.

That morning Paloma was in her robe, putting her closet in order. She had draped her innumerable dresses over the bed, the chairs, and the folding screen. She picked them up, examined them, smelled them, and put them down again, like I sometimes did with my books. When she saw me, she energetically spread out her most sinfully lavish outfits, perhaps to impress me. I remembered Angustias and felt depressed at the contrasting splendor of so many furs, silks, and feathers.

"What a face you've got on you!" Dolli exclaimed. "You look like you've been slapped!"

I couldn't contain myself, so I told them about Angustias' tribulations.

"She's a poor girl, but honorable," Encarnita sighed.

Paloma, however, made a joke out of it.

"If she'd do like we do, she wouldn't have anything to complain about."

I left discouraged. At one o'clock I ordered breakfast and stretched out for a nap. I slept for a long time because it was late afternoon when I woke up. Someone was knocking at the door. Paloma and Dolli came in.

"Poor girl!" Dolli said. "She refuses to eat anything and she's spent the whole afternoon closed up in her room."

At first, I didn't know who they were talking about.

"Encarnita says she can lend her a pair of shoes," Paloma intervened. "I can give her a dress and some jewelry. Did you say her boyfriend expects her at seven o'clock?"

Immediately I knew what was going on.

"Hurry up!" I exclaimed, getting off the bed. "You have less than an hour to convince her and get her dressed."

While Dolli and Paloma went to Angustias' room, I headed for the kitchen. In the hallway, the military man intercepted me. The news seemed to have spread through every nook and cranny of the boarding house.

"Did you hear the news?" he asked me. "She can't go to the party because she doesn't have a dress! If I wore skirts, I'd lend her one."

The young priest was excitedly running down the hall. "They've already gone into Angustias' room," he said. "I just saw them. I'll go listen to what they're saying."

Doña Candelas said as she passed: "And her father playing dominos! Besides that, he owes me three months rent."

The priest reappeared. "Now they're convincing her!"

"If she doesn't listen to them, we'll proceed *manu militari*," the officer advised. "I'll give the order to pick her up and between all of us we'll strip her down to her panties and stuff her in one of Paloma's dresses."

A little later we saw Paloma and Dolli pass by. Both gave us a wink. Angustias followed behind them, whining about the sleeve of her dress.

When Encarnita came a half hour later to tell us that "now she was ready," we shot out into the hall, went into the fragrant bedroom, and confirmed that our lowly boarding house had been visited by a queen. Angustias was in front of the mirror, coiffed, bedecked with jewelry, endlessly contemplating herself, still incredulous and teary, but radiant, and glowing with happiness. While Paloma finished taking the last stitches, Dolli fastened the necklace, and Encarnita got the gloves for her. After all the final touches were made, Angustias started for the front door with all of us following behind her. She had barely put her hand on the doorknob, however, when she abruptly turned around: "I'm not going!"

"Are you crazy?" Doña Candelas intervened.

"I'm not going!" Angustias repeated, raising her hands to her temples. All of us, talking at the same time, tried to persuade her.

"I'm not going! I'm not going, I'm not going, I'm not going . . . !"

And she didn't go. Her pride wouldn't allow her to go, even if her life depended on it.

LIMA, 1959

Painted Papers

I let Carmen talk while I sipped my Calvados[1] and secretly kept eyeing my watch. It was getting very late, and I was waiting for the right moment to tell her we should be leaving, we could be doing more interesting things than just sitting here on the mezzanine of the Danton Café, miserably wasting the best hours in idle talk, while all around us couples were kissing and, in the hotels of the district, thoughts were turning to love. But Carmen kept talking about the Spaniard who adored her, another who left after giving her a child; and I indignantly began to notice, between yawns and drinks, that it was four o'clock in the morning.

"I'll walk you to your hotel," I said, signaling the waiter.

"Of course," Carmen agreed, tilting her cheek for me to kiss.

The streets of the Latin Quarter were deserted at that hour. The anachronous, forsaken sound of New Orleans blues was coming from some bar. La Pérgola was doing business behind closed doors. As we passed the Metro Bar, we saw its doors opening to the early risers.

"Wait," Carmen said. "Do you mind if we take a stroll before going to the hotel?"

As we walked down Buci Street, she scurried ahead of me, while I impatiently followed behind. When she came to a store specializing in travel accessories, she stopped.

"Is anyone coming?" she asked, as she stretched her arms toward the display window and removed a travel poster in which you could barely make out a blue bay overshadowed by a volcano.

"I've had my eye on this one for a long time," she added, rolling it up and tucking it under her cloak. "Let's go to Seine Street in the Naples district. There's another one over there that interests me."

Without waiting for my reaction, she took out through the labyrinth of dark, narrow streets. I was feeling a bit lost like I always felt when I walked this district at night; my sense of direction was challenged by walks through the intricate network of streets that sprouted before the concept of urbanism came into existence. Streets that seemed to run parallel, began to separate and veer off toward diametrically opposite points; others, whose contiguity was inconceivable, suddenly intersected each

1. The name of a popular brandy-wine made from apples. It comes from Calvados, in the Normandy province of northwestern France.

other, made a loop, only then to come at each other head on and effect either a near miss or merge, losing their names to another artery.

Carmen reached Seine Street, hesitated for a moment, then went over to the side of a restaurant that featured a poster with a mountain motif. This time she yanked it down with one tug, after spotting two policemen on bicycles at the end of the street. Taking my arm, she told me to act as if nothing had happened, and we started walking toward the hotel.

With only three blocks left to go, she stopped a second time. "I forgot! Day before yesterday I saw a wall covered with posters near Luxembourg Gardens. They're new, with scenes of the Dalmatian coast. Let's go. We'll just look at them."

I protested, saying that it was going to be daylight soon, but Carmen took my arm and dragged me along Monsieur le Prince Street. When we passed in front of her hotel, I tried to stop her, but she promised we'd be on our way back within ten minutes.

There really was a wall plastered with new posters near Luxembourg. Carmen contemplated them for a moment; then, unable to contain herself, she began to remove them one at a time. Since there wasn't any more room for them under her cape, she handed me the roll.

"Put that on the ground. You pull them off, too. Help me!"

I snatched one poster just to please her, then another, and another, but dispassionately and disgusted by what seemed to me a defacement of city property.

"Now this is enough!" I complained. "What are you going to do with all this paper?"

Carmen kept on working, without giving me an answer. When the wall was stripped bare, we collected our spoils and started back. We had only taken ten steps, however, when Carmen stopped again.

"Now that we're here, we can skip over to Soufflot Street. There's a wealth of posters over there. You'll see."

It was useless persuading her not to go, so I followed her. Soufflot wasn't our only stop because after that we went to the Pantheon Plaza, down Cujas Street, took Sorbonne, and returned by way of Saint Germain Boulevard. At six in the morning, in full daylight, exhausted and livid, we arrived at the door of her hotel.

What I feared came true: "It's very late now to ask you in. The landlord must be up. It doesn't matter. We'll see each other tonight. You'll come by for me, right?"

At two in the morning I was in front of the small Arabic cabaret on Huchette Street, waiting for Carmen to come out. She had found a job there of a secret and diverse nature; she took the customers' coats at the door, sold cigarettes, waited tables, and, when invited, chatted with the lonely local patrons. When she saw me standing in the doorway, she collected her day's pay, picked up her pocketbook and cape, and hurriedly left.

She took my arm and we headed for Saint Michel Boulevard.

"Let's have a drink first," she said.

We passed in front of Cluny Café, the Old Navy, and the Mabillon, which were all closed by then. At Deux Magots the waiters were stacking the chairs. We ended up at Royal Saint Germain and ordered a beer. I was still in a bad mood.

"What's the matter?" Carmen asked me.

"Yesterday you kept me up all night long! I don't like spending an evening that way, walking like an idiot the entire night!"

Carmen started laughing. After she took a swig of beer, she became serious: "I'm a difficult woman. My friends have to get used to me."

Then she began telling the monotonous story of her misfortunes, of the men who had abandoned her, the years she couldn't leave Paris or the Latin Quarter, a son staying with a wet nurse in the countryside, memories of her childhood in Málaga, quarrels with the hotel landlords, trouble with the police. I was yawning shamelessly. There is nothing more boring to a man than listening to a woman he doesn't love telling him her intimate, sad stories.

"Let's go," I said, finally, and paid for the beers.

When we left, she suddenly stopped, indecisive, on the sidewalk. "This evening . . ." she began.

"Oh, no!" I protested. "You're not going to start in with the posters now!"

Carmen took me by the arm, pleaded with me, told me about the poster she had seen that afternoon near the School of Medicine, a wonderful poster of a blue sea and a heavenly coast.

"You're going to want to swipe it, aren't you?" I asked.

"Look at it first, then you decide!"

"Good-bye!" I responded sharply; then I turned around and started walking away. I heard Carmen's footsteps coming behind me. After about twenty steps, she caught up with me, and hung on my arm.

"This is the second time we've gone out! Just two times and you're ready to dump me. You're just like all the others!"

"Leave me alone!" I shouted.

But Carmen caught up with me again.

"All right," she said. "You can't understand these things! Let's go then, straight to my hotel."

Her promise brought me to my senses. As we walked, I explained the futility of wasting time that way, the risks involved in stealing public posters, the lack of civic pride she showed by constantly sabotaging municipal decor. Carmen listened to me silently, nodding her head in agreement.

When we reached Odeon Square, she stopped, sadly looked down the length of the boulevard toward the School of Medicine, and dragged me along Monsieur le Prince Street toward her hotel.

After cautiously closing the door, we tiptoed up the stairs, without lighting the stairway landings. We climbed and climbed up the stairs. I was suffocating in that black pit, blindly guided by Carmen's hand. Finally, we bumped into a wall.

"Here it is," she whispered, and with a nudge, she ushered me into another dark compartment and flicked on the light switch.

I was stunned. It looked more like the storage loft of a printing shop than a hotel room. There were sheets and sheets of paper. In fact, they were posters of every shape and size, some folded, others rolled, in piles or columns, jumbled, between the sparse pieces of furniture. Many were tacked to the wall, to the flat ceiling or to the window, making a shade of sorts. The bed was hardly visible under the deluge of papers.

"I have more in here," Carmen said, opening a wardrobe from which poured a pile of dusty posters. Then she bent down, put her hands under the bed and pulled out another pile.

While I was looking aghast at all this chaos, telling myself how many months and years it must have taken her to collect all those tangibles, how many sleepless nights, how many terrifying, cold mornings, Carmen was spreading the posters out for me to see.

"This is Rome! Can you see the dome of Saint Peter's Cathedral? Here are the windmills of Holland. Look, the Tower of London! The Parthenon in Greece . . ."

When I saw her face, I recoiled with surprise; her eyes had a dazzling, unreal glow to them; her nostrils were pulsating as she frantically panted; her lips were moving incessantly, uttering explanations sometimes sounding intelligent, but mechanical, like a rehearsed speech, while her arms tirelessly kept unfurling the pictures, letting them fall at her feet, creating a vortex of countrysides where Niagara Falls spilled over into the Buddhist temples of Indochina.

I was suddenly scared. Carmen's eyes were squinted and her breathing more rapid. I backed toward the door. Opening it abruptly, I made it to the hallway and raced down the dark stairs, not caring that the iron handrail was taking the skin off my hand.

Once I got to the street, I took off down Saint Germain Boulevard, confused, trying to calm down, knowing that I was running away, leaving my reasoning tumbling along behind, while my body dashed on ahead.

I hadn't recuperated yet when I saw something out of the corner of my eye that made me stop. There was a poster stuck on the door of a bookstore, not far from the School of Medicine. It was a poster of the Málaga coast, of Carmen's beloved coast; true, it was a poster like any other, but one that captivated me in a strange way. I looked at it with fascination, studying every detail, every artistic device used by the anonymous artist or the clever photographer who had applied his talent to opening a window of color onto the world of gray Parisian days. Only then did I understand what a travel poster meant to her. Each poster, any of them, was an escape, the distant country, the illusive city, the endlessly postponed vacation, the unattainable days of peace and tranquillity, the impossible trip, the scorned promise of exotic adventures, the consoling world of illusion. Hadn't Carmen simply replaced each of her dreams and frustrated plans with a collection of posters? For many years she'd been traveling around the world without ever leaving her neighborhood or her miserable hotel room, much like a child pouring over geography books by lamplight.

It was for that reason, or perhaps because of a childish whim, or a secret, repressed desire of mine, that I snatched the poster and hurried back to her hotel, thinking this picture would complete a circular, imaginary voyage; I hoped it would be the rare piece of the collection, the precious space of time granted to a desperate traveler, one more link in the chain of delirious acts, or perhaps, the last hellish journey, bringing to a close the circle of madness.

LIMA, 1960

CPSIA information can be obtained at www.ICGtesting.com
Printed in the USA
BVOW01s0707090614

355654BV00001B/10/P